AWESOME SPACE
FACTS
FOR KIDS

Discover Amazing Facts, Mind-Blowing Records, and the Wonders of the Universe!

John Hicks

FREE BONUS

SCAN TO GET OUR NEXT BOOK FOR FREE!

Table of Contents

INTRODUCTION

Outer space is a fascinating topic that's captured people's imaginations for thousands of years. From movies about alien invasions to true stories about landing on the moon, almost everyone on the planet has wondered about space at some point in their lives. Many of these modern ideas about space are influenced by ideas from the ancient world and the earliest discoveries about our universe.

Space is so important in our daily lives that you might not even realize how often you're talking about it. Do you know that you're bringing up objects from the solar system whenever you mention a day of the week? Though it may be hard to believe, in Latin, Tuesday is named after Mars and Wednesday is named after Mercury. Some space-related words even stick out after they're translated to English. *Monday* is actually a shorter version of "moon-day."

In this book, you'll find all sorts of fun facts about the history of space and how we explore the universe. We'll start by introducing planets, moons, black holes, and other fascinating parts of outer space. This will help you understand different parts of the solar system and how they all fit together.

From there, we'll discuss space exploration and unexplained mysteries that scientists hope to solve in the future. You'll learn all about the instruments and gadgets researchers use to study space, launch spacecraft, and support astronauts while they work far above Earth's surface. We'll also talk about some of the most impressive achievements in the history of space exploration.

We'll close out our time together by reviewing different activities and games you can enjoy if you want to learn more about space. The amazing part of space exploration is that there's always more to discover. Whether you want to be an astronaut, or you're just interested in learning about the inverse we live in, this book is the perfect way to get started.

WHAT IS SPACE?

Outer space starts approximately 62 miles above Earth's surface. Most of what we call "outer space" is completely empty in between objects, such as planets or stars. When scientists want to talk about all physical things in space at the same time, they use the term *celestial objects*.

Since everything is so spread out, the amount of light and heat are very different from one area to the next. That makes it hard to talk about space as a single place. It's like trying to describe the Earth when there's ice in one part and desert heat in another.

However, there are some facts that apply to every area. For example, space, as a whole, is silent for humans because there's nothing out there to carry sound as we know it. Some particles produce a certain kind of sound, but it's too quiet for humans to hear. However, satellites can detect these noises with special equipment.

Most of our research in space has been focused on our own galaxy, which we call the *Milky Way*. Since space is so big and spread out, scientists have divided the galaxy into four smaller pieces called *quadrants*. Having a way to map the galaxy makes it easier to understand where objects are located. There are potentially trillions of galaxies out there in the universe, and in the future, we may be able to explore other galaxies.

THE CHALLENGES OF SPACE

Throughout history, exploring new areas has never been easy. Studying space is especially tough because the conditions beyond our planet are so different than what we experience on Earth. Even reaching outer space requires some of the world's most advanced technology. Many of the booster rockets in use today are constantly being improved and upgraded.

Once materials are in space, the average temperature is 487 degrees Fahrenheit below freezing! For context, water freezes at 32 degrees, and the average temperature on the Earth's surface is 59 degrees. Because of this, spacecraft and other equipment must be covered in layers that hold in the heat. Since space is so empty that it hardly contains any matter or air, objects don't lose heat as quickly as they would on Earth. Robots, like the rovers used on Mars, can adjust their temperature based on whether they're too hot or cold on the surface.

Space is especially dangerous for astronauts. People who travel into space are under a lot of mental and physical stress. They have to deal with higher levels of radiation, which is a type of energy, and the lack of gravity. Plus, if anything goes wrong, astronauts are too far away for anyone on the ground to help.

Traveling into space is so difficult that multiple countries often work together. Teaming up with another space agency makes it easier to solve complicated problems and invent new equipment. It's also cheaper to pay for research if more than one country is willing to chip in.

ALIEN LIFE

One of the most interesting questions about space is whether there's the chance of finding other living creatures. The universe is so enormous that it's impossible to know for sure. In our solar system, Earth is the only planet that we know of that supports life. However, scientists continue to study planets outside our solar system to see if any show signs of water or basic life forms.

Even if there is life on other planets, there's no guarantee that those life forms will be advanced enough to communicate. Because of this, instead of waiting for another species to get in touch, researchers are constantly searching for other planets that *could* support life. Discovering water or certain types of gases on another planet besides Earth would make finding alien life far more likely.

Instead of space travel, some experts think it's better to focus on inventing tools that allow us to see farther into the universe. A powerful telescope would allow scientists to learn about other planets without actually having to go there. Traveling into space is expensive, and no one knows what will happen to equipment once it arrives at its destination. Exploring space with astronauts is even riskier, since many places are so far away it would take years — or even lifetimes—to reach them, and astronauts could run into trouble too far away to make it safely back to Earth.

THE SOLAR SYSTEM

Even though we're used to seeing the planets lined up in a row on drawings, there are actually huge pockets of open space in between each one. Earth and Neptune are almost 3 billion miles apart—and that's not even the full length of the solar system! That's why astronomers invented their own way of measuring distance based on how many miles are in between Earth and the sun.

A single astronomical unit (AU) equals 93 million miles. It would take an airplane over 20 years to cross that much space! Using AUs is simpler than writing out all those zeroes for every measurement. For example, Jupiter is 5.2 AU away from the sun, which is another way of saying 484,000,000 miles.

While you're learning about space, you might also see distances measured in *light-years*. A light-year is based on how far light can travel in a single year. Each light-year equals almost 6 trillion miles, so light-years are only used for things that are extremely far away.

PLANETS AND ATMOSPHERES

There hasn't always been a clear definition of what counts as a planet. Once scientists agreed on the definition, the number of planets in our solar system changed. We currently have eight planets in our solar system, but there used to be nine; Pluto was removed from the list in August 2006.

The four planets closest to the sun are Mercury, Venus, Earth, and Mars. They're known for being small and rocky. Larger planets such as Jupiter, Saturn, Uranus, and Neptune are farther away from the sun and made of gas. Jupiter is the biggest of all — it's so enormous that you could fit Earth inside of it 1,300 times before running out of room!

Each planet is surrounded by a bubble of gas called an *atmosphere*. On Earth, this extra layer around the planet holds in warmth and supplies the planet with enough oxygen to support plants, animals, and people. Different planets have different types of gases in their atmosphere. A human who traveled to Venus wouldn't be able to breathe because Venus's atmosphere is mostly carbon dioxide and nitrogen instead of oxygen.

Depending on where you live and the time of year, you can easily see five of the planets in our solar system from Earth: Mercury, Venus, Mars, Jupiter and Saturn. If you want to catch a glimpse of Uranus and Neptune, you'll need a telescope to help you see farther away. Many astronomers and other scientists who research the planets use powerful telescopes in dark parts of the world where they don't have to worry about lights from the city getting in the way.

SATELLITES AND MOONS

A *satellite* is an object in space that travels around a larger object, like a planet. The smaller object follows a path known as an *orbit*. All orbits are *elliptical*, which means shaped like an oval, but the shape and size vary. Think about the difference between a long, skinny oval and a shorter one that's wider in the middle. That's why some satellites take more time to complete a full orbit compared to others.

Satellites made by humans are launched into space to help people communicate and share information. However, there are also natural satellites. Moons fall into this category. Not every planet has the same number of moons. For instance, the Earth has one moon, Mercury and Venus don't have any, while Jupiter has close to 100! However, this number can change if moons break apart into multiple pieces or move away from the planet.

COMETS, ASTEROIDS, AND METEORS

Comets are made of dust and ice left behind after the solar system was formed — approximately 4.6 billion years ago. Asteroids are just as old as comets, but they're much larger and solid. Some asteroids also contain rare metals such as gold and platinum.

As a comet or asteroid gets closer to a star, such as our sun, the heat causes some of the ice to melt. The comet releases dust and pebble-sized rocks that eventually encounter planets like Earth. Small bits of debris may break free from asteroids, and these falling rocks create what we call shooting stars and meteor showers. Most meteors burn up before reaching the ground, so they don't pose a threat to anyone watching from the surface.

HOW WE EXPLORE SPACE

As you've already learned, it takes teamwork and dedication to make it into space. Space agencies like the National Aeronautics and Space Administration (NASA) hire all kinds of experts to design their missions. Engineers, doctors, and computer scientists play key roles in mapping out travel paths and making sure astronauts arrive safely at their destination.

ROCKET BOOSTERS

A *rocket booster* is what launches a spacecraft into the air. It's powered by special fuels like liquid oxygen and hydrogen that can produce enough energy to help a spacecraft escape Earth's gravity. A spacecraft that wants to enter space needs to be traveling at least 25,000 miles per hour! Without the help of a rocket booster, gravity would keep the spacecraft from breaking free from orbit.

RESEARCH SATELLITES

NASA and other agencies maintain a network of satellites that help scientists understand more about life on Earth. Satellites are able to see large areas of the planet all at once, including places that would be tough for researchers to visit in person. Some satellites also monitor conditions in space. The Deep Space Climate Observatory satellite does both.

Research satellites are often designed to do one specific job. The Ice, Cloud, Land and Elevation Satellite 2 (ICESat-2) was launched in 2018 to measure the height of ice and land along the surface. This satellite uses a laser that sends 10,000 pulses per second to take measurements on the ground. ICESat-2 has even found hidden lakes in Antarctica. This information allows experts to track climate change and study how the planet is changing.

SPACE PROBES

In addition to satellites that stay close to Earth, NASA also sends out space probes to learn more about the universe. A space probe doesn't have any humans on board, so it can travel farther than manned spacecraft. These probes contain specialized tools, sensors, and instruments to collect scientific data during their journeys and send this information back, even when they're far out in space or exploring the surface of another planet.

LIFE IN SPACE

Living and working in space isn't easy, and besides the people who actually go into space, NASA has over 18,000 employees who support each mission from the surface. These experts make sure astronauts are safe and comfortable during their time in space. They work through problems that would be too big for astronauts to solve on their own and provide advice for any issues that pop up unexpectedly.

BECOMING AN ASTRONAUT

Thousands of people apply to become an astronaut every year, but only a few are selected. In order to become an astronaut in the United States, you need to be a U.S. citizen and must prove that you have enough experience in subjects such as engineering and math. Applicants must also be healthy enough to complete training.

NASA hires astronauts approximately every four years. Thousands of people apply, but only a few make the cut. In 2020, only 10 people were hired—out of 12,000 applicants. If your dream is to one day become an astronaut, however, don't let these numbers discourage you! Even though the odds of being selected aren't high, studying valuable subjects, such as physics, and working hard in school make it more likely that you'll be chosen.

Working for NASA as an astronaut used to be the only way to visit space. However, in recent years, companies that aren't part of the government have created their own rockets and spacecraft. These companies have their own rules about who can go into space as a tourist. Since passengers are only buying a ticket for a short trip, the limits for age and health aren't as strict.

SPACE STATIONS

There are currently two space stations in low orbit over Earth. The first is Tiangong Space Station, which belongs to China. The second is the International Space Station (ISS), where astronauts from 15 countries work together. Other space stations have existed in the past, and more are supposed to be added in the future.

Astronauts have continuously lived onboard the International Space Station since November 2000. Studying the astronauts on these stations has allowed researchers to learn more about how the human body reacts to being in space. This information is important for planning future missions and longer journeys outside of Earth's orbit.

THE HISTORY
OF SPACE

In the past, researchers didn't have a way to observe distant parts of the solar system. They relied on their eyes to study the stars and understand where the Earth fit in the universe. Unsurprisingly, they didn't always come up with the right answer. Plenty of theories were ruled out later, once people had access to more modern tools like telescopes.

Regardless, the study of space has always required teamwork. Even as far back as the 1600s, experts from different countries shared theories and built upon ideas from the ancient world. They used what they knew to create new inventions and write books about the universe, paving the way for modern astronauts.

However, studying space from the surface isn't the same as exploring it in person. Since humans can only spend short periods in outer space, it's taken a long time to learn basic details about new parts of the solar system. As technology becomes more advanced, it will get easier to reach distant areas and research places that have yet to be discovered.

THE ANCIENT WORLD

Astronomy, or the scientific study of space, started a long time ago. Ancient civilizations like the Mayans built observatories in present-day Central America to watch the movements of the sun, moon, and other celestial objects. They were able to predict how planets moved and when celestial events—like eclipses—would take place. These calculations were remarkably accurate for their time.

In northern Egypt, a mathematician named Eratosthenes was the first person to estimate the size of the entire planet around the year 240 BCE. It all started when Eratosthenes heard a story from travelers who had been to the town of Syene. They said that sunlight completely filled a well at noon on the summer solstice, when the sun was directly overhead.

Eratosthenes decided to measure the shadow cast by the sun at the same time of year in Alexandria. It was close to 1/50 of a circle. Once he had that measurement, he realized he could estimate the size of the Earth by figuring out the distance between Syene and Alexandria and multiplying it by 50.

Many ancient cultures also worshipped the sun as a god. Ancient Egyptians believed that the sun god Ra wore the sun on his headdress and carried the sun across the sky in a boat. Meanwhile, in the area that would later become Mexico, the Aztecs thought the world would end if darkness defeated the sun god Huītzilōpōchtli. Because of this, they offered sacrifices to Huītzilōpōchtli to ensure he was powerful enough to continue the battle.

THE MIDDLE AGES

During medieval times, universities required students to learn about astronomy. Schools felt that astronomy was just as important as math, grammar, and music. Many people also thought that the position of objects in space could affect what happened on Earth. They followed the position of the sun and planets in the sky and used that information to predict what might happen in the future. This practice is called *astrology*.

You might have already heard of astrology and looked up your zodiac sign. For example, according to western astrology, if you were born between October 23 and November 21, you're a Scorpio. People who study astrology believe that when you are born affects your personality. Scorpios, for instance, are known for being strong and independent.

The modern zodiac has 12 signs in total. This system is different from the Chinese zodiac, which features 12 animals based on the

Chinese calendar. In this system, each year receives its own sign. The year 2000 started off the new millennium with a dragon. In Chinese culture, the dragon is considered a sign of good luck and success.

THE RENAISSANCE

The Renaissance took place between 1450 and 1650. During that time, Europeans were especially interested in science, art, and geography. There were also major discoveries about outer space, thanks to thinkers like Polish mathematician Nicolaus Copernicus, who questioned ancient Greek ideas about the planets.

Copernicus had a theory that the Earth wasn't the center of the universe. That might seem obvious now, but people in the ancient world thought the sun revolved around the Earth, not the other way around. Other astronomers doubted Copernicus — at least until the early 1600s, when the Italian scientist Galileo Galilei started conducting research of his own.

In 1609, Galileo heard about a type of telescope and decided to build his own. The first one he created made objects look three times bigger than what he could see with just his eyes. Over time, he improved the telescope until it could make objects appear 30 times larger. At the time, most people who had telescopes wanted to use them for military battles or navigation. However, Galileo used his telescope to study space.

In his studies, Galileo discovered that the moon isn't smooth, as most people thought at the time, but has craters and pits instead.

He also observed the planets and realized that their appearance changes, just like the moon. Sometimes, Venus would be a full circle, but it didn't always stay that way. Before this, no one had ever been able to see the planet well enough to tell that its shape was different.

Galileo's telescope wasn't powerful enough to see the dozens of moons around Jupiter, but he was able to study four of the largest ones. Io, Ganymede, Europa, and Callisto are part of a group named the "Galilean moons" to honor his discovery. Based on what he learned from Jupiter's moons, Galileo agreed with Copernicus's theory that the sun was the center of the solar system — after all, if everything in space revolved around the Earth, other planets wouldn't have moons of their own.

Meanwhile, Danish astronomer Tycho Brahe and his German assistant Johannes Kepler measured and charted how other planets moved. Kepler came up with three laws of planetary motion and agreed with Copernicus about the position of the sun. He was also the first person to discover that planets don't orbit the sun in an exact circle.

MODERN TIMES

Modern space exploration started with the "Space Race" between the United States and the Soviet Union. These two major world powers each wanted to prove that they were better, smarter, and more advanced than the other. On October 4, 1957, the Soviet Union launched the first human-made satellite into orbit. Since tensions were already high for political and military reasons, this was a major event.

The competition between the United States and the Soviet Union led to inventions and scientific methods that are still in use today. The moon landing in 1969 was just the beginning. Since then, space agencies have sent probes to Mars, identified planets outside our solar system, and tracked a meteoroid before it hit the Earth. In 2019, researchers at the Event Horizon Telescope Collaboration even figured out how to take a picture of a black hole.

NASA's future goals include sending astronauts to Mars and exploring various areas of the moon. It will also continue monitoring how the Earth changes over time. This information will help scientists understand how to protect people, animals, and the environment.

CHAPTER ONE: THE SUN AND STARS

The sun, sometimes called *Sol*, is a perfect example of nature's power. It's the center of our Solar System and a key part of what allowed life to develop on Earth. Without the light and warmth from the sun, our planet wouldn't have evolved into what it is today. Even though the sun seems like it's one of a kind, it's actually one star among many. A star is considered a sun when planets revolve around it.

So far, NASA has found over 3,200 stars with planets orbiting around them. Some solar systems have more than one sun; in fact, it's actually more common for suns to appear together. That could change, though, as scientists figure out how to look farther outside our solar system and study distant locations.

OUR SUN

The sun was created, along with the rest of our solar system, about 4.6 billion years ago. Dust and gas came together in a cloud to create a *solar nebula*. The nebula kept rotating faster and faster until it collapsed and formed a disk. Most of that material was used to create the sun. Because the solar system has so much empty space, the sun makes up 99.8% of all mass within it! The rest of the planets are part of the remaining 0.2%.

The sun is 864,000 miles in diameter. *Diameter* is measured straight through the middle, so that isn't the same as measuring all the way around the outside. In total, the sun is 109 times as wide as the Earth. That might seem huge, but when you zoom out and look at other stars, the sun is only average in size—the largest stars ever found can be up to 100 times larger!

The outer part of the sun is called the *corona*. On the surface, the sun is 10,000 degrees Fahrenheit. The temperature increases as it gets closer to the core, where it can reach up to 27 million degrees Fahrenheit! For comparison, liquid lava from Hawaiian volcanoes is only 2,200 degrees Fahrenheit.

In addition to heat, the sun's corona also releases gas and particles in a form of wind. This solar wind contains particles that are charged with electricity, which can travel at speeds of nearly a million miles per hour as they move away from the sun. Luckily, Earth's magnetic field and atmosphere protect the planet from most of the effects of solar wind.

However, there are certain times when this solar wind gets much stronger. Solar storms can form quickly, without giving a lot of warning. During solar storms, the sun experiences *solar flares*, or short bursts of intense radiation, and releases more energy into the solar system than usual. The increase in radiation can damage materials in space and pose a danger to astronauts. Because of this risk, scientists use satellites to keep an eye on solar weather and make predictions about when a storm might happen.

WHAT ARE STARS?

Stars are made of gases like hydrogen and helium. These gases burn and release energy as heat and light. The sun is the closest star to Earth, but there are billions of other stars spread throughout the universe. They come in a variety of shapes and sizes, so no two stars are exactly alike. They may also transform into different types of stars throughout their lifespan.

TEMPERATURE

Stars are graded according to their temperatures using letters such as *O, B, A, F, G, K*, and *M*. The hottest stars are assigned the letter *O*, while the coldest ones are marked as *M*. The sun in our solar system has a rating of *G*, so it's average in terms of warmth. A star's color will also vary based on its temperature; hotter stars appear white or blue, and cooler ones are red.

TYPES OF STARS

Stars fall into four main categories: *main sequence, giants, supergiants*, and *white dwarfs*. They're sorted based on their color, temperature, brightness, and other qualities. Most stars fall into the main sequence. They stay in this group for approximately 5 billion years while they're still stable.

Once stars start to die, they use up their hydrogen, and their outer layers begin expanding. Over time, they become giants or supergiants. These stars aren't growing because they're gaining material—they're just stretching out to fill more space. Some supergiants are up to 1,500 times as wide as the sun!

Eventually, stars in this group will explode and become nebulas or supernovas. From there, they transition into black holes, neutron stars, or white dwarfs, depending on how much matter is in the star. *Matter* is a term that describes any material that takes up space and has weight. Living creatures, items, and even air are made up of matter. The amount of matter in an object is called its *mass*.

There's also a theory that white dwarfs go through one last stage in their life cycle. Some scientists believe that white dwarfs turn into *black* dwarfs once they stop giving off heat and light. If that's true, then black dwarfs are just too cold and dark to see, so the only way to find them is by seeing how gravity behaves around them. If other objects are pulled toward a spot in space that looks empty, it could actually contain a black dwarf.

STAR CONSTELLATIONS

Constellations are groups of stars that form recognizable shapes and patterns. For example, most people know how to find the *Big Dipper*, which looks like a ladle, in the night sky. Stars in the same constellation often seem close together, but they usually only appear that way from Earth's surface. In reality, stars in the same constellation may not be anywhere near each other.

Because of how the Earth orbits the sun, not all constellations are visible at the same time in the same place. A person in one country could have a totally different view of the stars than someone halfway around the world. Your view of constellations will also change slightly from night to night. If you're used to searching for the same constellation, you'll need to keep turning toward to the west to find it.

Finding new constellations was popular in ancient times. Many constellations are named after animals, people, and everyday items. There are currently 88 official constellations, but there's nothing to stop you from inventing your own! If you see a spot where multiple stars can connect to form a particular object or creature, you can make that your own personal constellation.

FAMOUS CONSTELLATIONS

The *Big Dipper* is actually a part of two constellations: *Ursa Major* and *Ursa Minor*. Their names translate to "Great Bear" and "Little Bear." *Ursa Major* is especially important because the two stars on the end of the *Big Dipper* can be used to find the North Star. The North Star, which is officially named *Polaris*, helps people navigate when they don't have a compass or other tools.

The constellation *Cassiopeia* is another popular constellation for navigation since it's visible all year in the Northern Hemisphere. It's shaped like either the letter *W* or *M*, depending on where it is in the sky. *Cassiopeia* is named for Andromeda's mother in Greek mythology. The legend is that, when Cassiopeia claimed that her daughter was even more beautiful than the sea nymphs, Poseidon sent a monster to attack Cassiopeia's people. Then, the hero Perseus rescued Andromeda and turned Cassiopeia into stars.

In the Southern Hemisphere, the most well-known constellation is the *Southern Cross*. The *Southern Cross* includes four stars in the shape of a cross with a smaller fifth star off to one side. Early explorers like Captain James Cook relied on this unique constellation to sail long distances. In modern times, it's become a symbol of pride for countries in the Southern Hemisphere — the *Southern Cross* even appears on several flags, including the ones for Australia and New Zealand.

NEBULAE AND GALAXIES

You've probably already heard small units within a whole referred to as "building blocks" — the body is made up of cells, physical objects are made up of atoms, and even places as gigantic as the universe rely on building blocks. Without galaxies and nebulae, the universe wouldn't have enough material and space to keep evolving over time.

NEBULAE AND NEW STARS

If you consider life on Earth and its environment, you'll realize that they usually follow a pattern or cycle. Think about water and rain; rain falls to the surface and gathers in puddles, lakes, and other bodies of water. Some of it evaporates and gathers to form new clouds, which eventually produce rain that sends the water back toward the surface.

Space has patterns and cycles, too. When a star dies, it explodes and throws gas and dust into space. Then, the leftover material clumps together in a cloud to form a nebula. Over the course of millions of years, the nebula can begin to form a new star. Thanks to modern technology, it's now possible to watch this process from a distance.

One of the best places to see stars forming is the *Eagle Nebula*. This nebula is about 5,700 light-years from Earth in the *Serpens* constellation. It was discovered in 1745 by the Swiss astronomer Jean-Philippe Loys de Cheseaux, and an American scientist named Edward Barnard photographed the nebula for the first time in 1895. Unlike many objects in space, the *Eagle Nebula* is visible with a basic telescope or pair of binoculars.

GALAXIES OF THE UNIVERSE

Galaxies are made of dust, gas, stars, and entire solar systems. Gravity holds all these different parts together. Our galaxy is the *Milky Way*, but there could be trillions of other galaxies out there in the universe. When scientists studied just one small part of space for 12 days, they found 10,000 galaxies.

The *Milky Way* is shaped like a spiral, but not all galaxies have the same appearance. Some even look like blobs, without a clear shape. Each galaxy is lit by the stars inside it, so if most of the stars are blue, the galaxy will look blue too.

BLACK HOLES

Black holes are formed by dying stars. Black holes collect mass in an extremely small area, the center of which is called a *singularity*, and the gravity in a black hole is so strong that not even light can escape. To get an idea of what a black hole is like, imagine fitting enough mass to make ten million suns into a spot as tiny as the tip of a pencil!

In 2015, experts used what they already knew about the universe to estimate the number of black holes. It's possible there are up to 40 *quintillion* black holes — that's the same as writing out 40,000,000,000,000,000,000! *Gaia BH1* is the closest black hole to Earth. It's located in the *Ophiuchus* constellation about 1,560 light-years away.

PHOTOGRAPHING A BLACK HOLE

In 2019, Dr. Katie Bouman and her team at the Event Horizon Telescope Collaboration took a picture of a black hole for the first time in history. Instead of trying to invent one telescope that was powerful enough to take the picture, the group connected eight separate telescopes. The same technique has allowed researchers to observe spacecraft and look at objects farther out in the universe.

The Event Horizon Telescope Collaboration placed telescopes in locations as far apart as Chile and Antarctica, and over 200 scientists worked together on the project. The data they collected was stored on hundreds of different hard drives, which then had to be transported to specialized centers in places like Boston. It took all kinds of experts and support staff to create the final photograph. Their success story is yet another example of why teamwork is so important in a complicated field like astronomy.

CHAPTER TWO: PLANETS AND MOONS

Our solar system contains eight planets, but there are likely trillions of other planets throughout the universe. Technology has developed enough to find other planets in the *Milky Way*, but looking at planets beyond our galaxy is far more challenging. Currently, scientists believe there's at least one planet for each star in the universe.

THE INNER PLANETS

The four planets closest to the sun are known as either the *inner planets* or the *rocky planets*. Earth is part of this category, even though Mercury, Venus, and Mars have different atmospheres and appearances. As a group, the inner planets are smaller than other planets like Jupiter or Saturn. They also have solid crusts that are mostly made up of metal and rock.

MERCURY: THE SWIFT PLANET

Mercury is the smallest planet in the solar system, at only 3,032 miles in diameter. In other words, it's about one third the size of Earth. Most of the planet's core is made up of iron. The surface also has sulfur and magnesium. Some scientists believe that another object crashed into Mercury while it was forming and tore off the outer layers. That would explain why so much of the planet is taken up by the metal core.

As the planet closest to the sun, Mercury's surface is exposed to extremely high temperatures on one side. Its atmosphere is only about 1% as thick as Earth's, so it doesn't have as much protection from the sun's heat or the coldness of space. The side that faces the sun can get as hot as 900 degrees Fahrenheit, while the other size falls as low as negative 300 degrees Fahrenheit.

Mercury is also known as the "Swift Planet" because it completes a full rotation around the sun in 88 days, which is faster than any other planet in our solar system. It travels at a speed of 105,947 miles per hour. In a race with Earth, Mercury would complete more than four laps before Earth could circle the sun one time.

VENUS: THE MORNING STAR

Venus is the closest planet to Earth, and they're both about the same size. From Earth, Venus is the brightest object in the sky besides the moon. That's how it earned the nickname "Morning Star," even though it isn't technically a star.

Venus has an iron core and a rocky crust. Learning about Venus is a challenge because of its thick atmosphere. Most of the atmosphere is made up of carbon dioxide, the same gas that increases the temperature on Earth. The atmosphere traps so much heat that Venus is the hottest planet in the solar system. It has an average temperature of 867 degrees Fahrenheit.

Because the atmosphere is so hot and dangerous, it's hard for spacecraft to survive for long on the surface. The Soviet Union sent the *Venera 7* probe to Venus in 1970, but its parachute ripped on the way down. It was damaged before reaching the surface and only sent data for 23 minutes. It was the first time in history any nation had managed to land on Venus and return information to Earth.

However, it isn't cheap to launch space probes, so it doesn't always make sense to land them on the surface if they're going to be destroyed almost immediately. Instead, other space agencies have sent probes to look at Venus from farther away. An American space probe named *Magellan* took images of the surface from 1990 to 1994. Next, the European Space Agency launched the *Venus Express* in 2005 to continue studying the surface and the planet's atmosphere, and the *Venus Express* is still in orbit to this day.

EARTH: THE BLUE PLANET

Obviously, it's much easier to study Earth than other planets — we're already on the surface! Earth is the largest of the inner planets and the third one from the sun. The Earth's core is made of mostly iron and nickel, and the outer crust consists of the various rocks and minerals we see around us every day.

Earth is unique because of its ability to support life. The atmosphere is 78% nitrogen, 21% oxygen, and 1% other gases. This combination is just right to allow plants and animals to survive. The atmosphere also causes sunlight to appear bluer in color. Combined with the blue oceans that make up over 70% of the planet's surface, it's understandable that Earth is known as the "Blue Planet."

MARS: THE RED PLANET

Mars is about half the size of Earth, and both planets are mostly made of materials that came from the inner part of the solar system. Mars is approximately 90 million years older than Earth because it didn't take as long to form. Earth and Mars are also the only inner planets to have moons. Mars has two: *Phobos* and *Deimos*.

Mars is known as the "Red Planet" because of how much iron oxide it has on the surface. Iron oxide is what causes rust to look red. Dust from the surface of Mars even makes the sky appear pink! Mars has giant craters and contains the biggest mountain in the solar system, Olympus Mons. For comparison, this mountain is over twice as tall as Mount Everest!

Scientists are especially interested in Mars because there's evidence of water forming throughout the planet. The atmosphere is 95% carbon dioxide, but it also contains approximately 1% water vapor. Additionally, rovers have found signs of water on the surface. This could mean that Mars might eventually evolve to support life. However, life forms that could survive on Mars would probably look much different than the life on Earth.

THE GAS GIANTS

After the inner planets, the next four planets are *gas giants*. Gas giants have a solid core surrounded by gases like hydrogen and helium. In our solar system, this category includes Jupiter, Saturn,

Uranus, and Neptune. Even though they belong to the same overall group, each planet has its own unique features.

JUPITER: THE GAS GIANT

Jupiter's nickname is simply the "Gas Giant" — it's famous for being the largest planet in the solar system. It's about 89,000 miles wide, making it bigger than all the other planets in our solar system combined. Jupiter also has the shortest day, since it rotates faster than other planets; a day on Jupiter only lasts for 10 hours.

Different parts of Jupiter's surface are covered in yellow, brown, white, and red clouds. From a distance, these clouds make it look like Jupiter has stripes. Jupiter is also home to the Great Red Spot, a huge storm that's even bigger than the Earth. The winds on Jupiter can reach speeds of over 400 mph.

Scientists are still learning about Jupiter. Since Jupiter's three rings are only made up of tiny bits of dust, it took until 1979 for NASA to discover them. Since astronomers on Earth weren't able to see them, the *Voyager 1* spacecraft discovered the rings as it was flying by Jupiter.

SATURN: THE RINGED PLANET

Saturn is the sixth planet from the sun, and it's about 750 times bigger than Earth. As a fellow gas giant, its atmosphere is similar to Jupiter's. Saturn is surrounded by more moons than any other planet in our solar system. It has 146 moons that we know of, but it's possible there are even more that have yet to be found.

Saturn is known as the "Ringed Planet" because it has seven distinct rings made of ice and rock. The rings are so large that Galileo was able to see them during the 1600s using one of history's earliest telescopes. Astronomers think the rings are made of pieces of asteroids and comets that broke apart before they reached the surface of the planet.

URANUS: THE ICE GIANT

Uranus is known as the "Ice Giant." Up to 80 percent of the planet is made of water, methane, and ammonia that scientists believe were originally ice when the planet first formed. Over time, the ice melted into liquid. The atmosphere around the core contains hydrogen, helium, and methane, and the methane is what causes Uranus to appear blue.

Like Saturn, Uranus has rings, and the outer ones are easier to see since they're brighter. However, Uranus is a bit unusual — it rotates in the opposite direction than all other planets in the solar system except Venus. It's also the only planet to spin on its side. It's possible that another object hit Uranus and changed the way it rotates.

At its closest point, Uranus is 1.6 billion miles from Earth. That makes it extremely challenging to study. So far, only the *Voyager 2* probe has been able to travel the distance to learn more. The *Voyager 2* was so far away that it took 18.5 hours for an instruction from Earth to reach the probe.

NEPTUNE: THE BLUE GIANT

Neptune is the farthest planet from the sun, and it was the last to be discovered by astronomers. The English astronomer John Couch Adams predicted there was another planet beyond Uranus in 1846, and a French mathematician named Urbain Jean Joseph Le Verrier published a similar theory around the same time. Their ideas were later proven correct when German astronomer Johann Gottfried Galle and his assistant Henrich Louis d'Arrest saw Neptune for the first time while working at the Berlin Observatory.

As a planet, Neptune is similar to Uranus since its atmosphere contains helium, hydrogen, and methane. Even though Uranus is also blue, Neptune is nicknamed the "Blue Giant" because its color is stronger. Neptune's surface is dark and extremely windy, with temperatures reaching 300 degrees Fahrenheit below freezing.

Voyager 2 visited Neptune in August 1989 and sent back images of the planet. To avoid getting pulled into Neptune's orbit, the probe took pictures from approximately 330,000 miles away. It also took pictures of some of Neptune's 16 moons before continuing its journey through the solar system.

DWARF PLANETS AND ASTEROIDS

Dwarf planets are similar to the main eight planets, but they don't meet all the requirements to be a full planet. The International

Astronomical Union (IAU) recognizes five dwarf planets in our solar system: *Pluto, Eris, Ceres, Makemake,* and *Haumea.*

Astronomers are still learning about these smaller celestial bodies. NASA's *Dawn* spacecraft studied the asteroid *Vesta* for over a year before starting its orbit of Ceres in March 2015. It spent over three years analyzing Ceres, making it the first spacecraft to ever orbit two different celestial bodies.

The *Voyager* 2 probe that visited Neptune in 1989 wasn't able to fly by Pluto. Because of this, Pluto wasn't photographed up close until July 14, 2015, when the *New Horizons* spacecraft arrived. *New Horizons* took pictures of Pluto and its five moons before moving on.

THE CONTROVERSY OVER PLUTO

Pluto is the most famous dwarf planet, as it was once considered the ninth planet in our solar system. Scientists decided it didn't qualify in 2006 after the IAU agreed on what counts as a planet. Believe it or not, there wasn't an official definition before that time. Pluto was downgraded to a dwarf planet and the asteroid Ceres was promoted to dwarf planet.

Many people were upset to learn that Pluto was no longer considered a full planet. However, the new definition says that a planet must orbit the sun, have a round shape, and clear the "neighborhood" around its orbit — which means it must be big enough to absorb or move smaller objects in its path. Pluto shares some of the space around its orbit with other objects of similar size, so it only meets the first two requirements. Since Pluto is already fully formed, it's unlikely to ever clear the area and regain its status as a planet.

However, the IAU's definition could still change at a later date. Not all scientists agree with their decision. Some experts think the definition of a planet should include any round object that orbits the sun and has a surface that's still changing. Under those requirements, Pluto and many other asteroids, dwarf planets, and moons would count as planets.

ASTEROIDS

Asteroids are small objects that were left behind when the solar system formed. Most asteroids in our solar system are located in the asteroid belt in between Mars and Jupiter. Asteroids can be divided into these three groups based on how they're formed:

- C-type asteroids are made of clay and silicate rock. They're darker than other types of asteroids. Up to 75% of our solar system's asteroids fall into this category.

- S-type asteroids contain stony materials, nickel, and iron. They may appear slightly green or red. Approximately 17% of our solar system's asteroids are S-type.

- M-type asteroids are metallic. They're mostly composed of nickel and iron, but they may also contain small amounts of gold, rhodium, platinum, and other rare metals.

Several space agencies have studied asteroids and sent spacecraft to fly past them. NASA's *Galileo* was the first, studying the Gaspara asteroid in October 1991 and Ida in August 1993. The European Space Agency later sent its *Rosetta* space probe to investigate the Steins asteroid in 2008 and the Lutetia asteroid in 2010.

Japan's *Hayabusa* was the first spacecraft to land on an asteroid and collect samples. It returned from its journey in 2010. The *Hayabusa 2* was launched at the end of 2014 to bring back samples from a different asteroid, and it completed its mission in December 2020. NASA is currently using the *OSIRIS-REx* to visit asteroids. The first U.S. collection of samples was delivered in September 2023.

COMETS

Comets are made of dust, ice, and rock. They have long tails that follow behind them as they move. Some comets are located in the Kuiper Belt beyond Neptune. They're considered short-period comets because it takes less than 200 years for them to complete a full orbit around the sun. There are also long-period comets from the Oort Cloud on the very edge of our solar system. Those comets can take up to 250,000 years to travel around the sun.

In some cases, gravity from a celestial body like a planet will pull a comet away from the Kuiper Belt or the Oort Cloud. These comets develop new orbits that look like long ovals. As they move toward the sun, they become more visible from Earth's surface. Some comets that travel to the inner part of the solar system will crash into the sun instead of circling around it.

MOONS OF THE SOLAR SYSTEM

Moons are a type of natural satellite. According to NASA, there are currently 293 different moons in our solar system. Only six of the main planets have at least one moon, but the number per planet varies widely.

Here's the exact number by planet:

- Mercury: 0

- Venus: 0

- Earth: 1

- Mars: 2

- Jupiter: 95

- Saturn: 146

- Uranus: 28

- Neptune: 16

- Pluto: 5

Even though Pluto isn't considered a main planet anymore, it still has five moons that count toward the total. It's possible there are other moons in our solar system that have yet to be found. In fact, three more moons were discovered around Jupiter in 2022.

EARTH'S MOON

Even though it looks close from the surface, Earth's moon is about 238,855 miles away! It would take a chain of 30 Earths to reach the moon. Over time, the moon has slowly pulled away from the Earth. It moves about one inch further away per year.

From Earth, the moon is the brightest object in space. Besides providing light, the moon helps the Earth stay stable instead of wobbling. Without the moon, weather would be unpredictable since the planet could turn in unusual ways. The moon also creates tides that support animal life in the ocean and clear pollution from the water.

The moon doesn't have enough atmosphere to prevent other objects from crashing into it. Asteroids, comets, and meteoroids have all struck the surface at different points in history—that's why the moon has so many craters. Tycho Crater, for example, is over 52 miles across at its widest point.

UNIQUE MOONS

Many moons in our solar system have special features that make them stand out from the pack. They weren't all created in the same areas or under the same conditions, so it makes sense that they have their own quirks. Here's a list of our solar system's most unique moons:

- Jupiter's moon *Io* is covered in hundreds of volcanoes. The pull of gravity between Jupiter, Io, and its other moons is so strong that the height of Io's surface can change by as much as 330 feet. Additionally, volcanic eruptions can send lava spraying miles into the air.

- *Phobos* is one of the two small moons that orbit Mars. Scientists believe the pull of gravity will eventually break Phobos into pieces.

- Neptune's largest moon, *Triton*, orbits the planet in the opposite direction. This is known as a *retrograde orbit*.

- *Atlas*, one of Saturn's many moons, is interesting because it's shaped like a flying saucer.

EXOPLANETS

Exoplanets are planets that orbit other stars besides the sun. It's difficult for astronomers to see exoplanets because they're often blocked out by the light from stars. Instead, scientists use other methods, such as seeing whether any stars look a bit shaky, since stars with planets in orbit don't rotate perfectly in balance.

Another way to find exoplanets is by waiting for a planet to cross in front of a star. The planet will create a dark spot that makes it easier to see. This at least gives astronomers enough information to learn about the size and shape of the object. Think of it like holding your hand in front of a light to make shadow puppets on the wall.

Space agencies like NASA are especially interested in finding exoplanets that could support life. The universe is so enormous that no one knows whether there could be another Earth-like planet out there orbiting a distant star.

SEARCHING FOR NEW EXOPLANETS

In 2009, NASA launched the Kepler Space Telescope to search for new exoplanets. It was able to find 2,681 confirmed exoplanets and 2,899 potential exoplanets in our galaxy. Astronomers who studied the data collected by the Kepler Space Telescope estimate that up to half of all the stars visible from Earth's surface may have planets in an area where water could form. That could be an important clue about where to find life outside our solar system.

The Kepler Space Telescope's mission ended in 2018, but scientists haven't finished learning about exoplanets. The Transiting Exoplanet Survey Satellite is still hard at work analyzing the sky to discover even more about the planets orbiting distant stars.

CHAPTER THREE:
SPACE EXPLORATION

When ancient civilizations studied the stars, they probably never imagined we'd have the technology to actually visit space in person. From doctors to mathematicians, it's taken experts from all kinds of different fields to create space programs capable of launching spacecraft into orbit. A goal as complicated as exploring the universe requires teamwork, dedication, and more than a little bit of luck.

THE SPACE RACE

The "Space Race" started during the Cold War between the United States, the Soviet Union, and their allies. The United States wanted to spread democracy, while the Soviet Union believed Communism was a better system of government. Unlike other wars in history, the Cold War didn't involve battles or armies. Instead, it was a period of political tension where the countries involved tried to show they were better than their opponents.

MAJOR GOALS

The Soviet Union put pressure on the United States and its allies when it sent the first manmade satellite into orbit in 1957. At that point, NASA didn't even exist! The United States was at risk of falling behind if they didn't work to keep up with the Soviet Union's scientific and military programs.

The next goal was to put an astronaut into space for the first time. The Soviet Union beat the United States again when they sent Yuri Gagarin into orbit on April 12, 1961. The American astronaut Alan

Shepherd followed on May 6, but he didn't complete a full orbit of the Earth. The United States didn't accomplish that until February 20, 1962, when John Glenn circled the planet aboard the *Friendship 7* spacecraft.

No matter how anyone measured it, the Soviet Union was far ahead of the United States. By mid-1962, America was desperate for a win to show they were still in the Space Race, so President John F. Kennedy came up with the next target. In May, he made a speech to Congress and said the United States should try to land on the moon before the end of the decade. Achieving this amazing feat would show the Soviet Union once and for all that America's space program was the best in the world.

THE MOON LANDING

Leaders in the U.S. government understood that beating the Soviet Union to the moon would require a special team. To that end, NASA established the Apollo program in 1961 to put all the best minds to work on space exploration. Before NASA could send anyone to the moon, they needed to invent the right equipment to keep a team of astronauts safe that far from Earth.

In 1967, a deadly accident, involving three members of *Apollo I* crew, reminded everyone involved that real people were putting their lives on the line to do something that had never been accomplished before. After sending *Apollo 7* into space in 1968, astronauts reached the moon for the first time aboard *Apollo 8*. However, the team only orbited the moon instead of landing. The next two missions tested more of the equipment astronauts would need to land on the surface and take off again for the journey home.

Finally, it was time for *Apollo 11* to attempt a moon landing. On July 20, 1969, Neil Armstrong became the first person to walk on the moon. He was soon joined by his crewmate Buzz Aldrin. Together, they collected samples of rock and dust to bring home for testing. Before departing for Earth, they left behind an American flag. Despite a strong start to its space program, the Soviet Union never managed to land on the moon.

SPACE AGENCIES

Governments around the world maintain their own space agencies. These groups are responsible for planning missions, conducting research, and exploring space. Some space agencies only belong to one country, while others are made up of multiple smaller countries from the same area. Space agencies can either carry out missions on their own or work together on shared projects.

THE NATIONAL AERONAUTICS AND SPACE ADMINISTRATION

In the 1950s, it was clear that the United States needed an agency to study outer space. The National Advisory Committee for Aeronautics already existed, but it only focused on flights that took place on Earth. President Dwight D. Eisenhower signed the National Aeronautics and Space Act to take the next step toward space exploration on July 29, 1958. After months of planning, NASA was officially created on October 1, with Dr. T. Keith Glennan as its first leader.

Today, NASA is a thriving organization with 10 field centers. These facilities each have their own responsibilities and tasks. For instance, the Jet Propulsion Laboratory in California builds advanced robots and sends probes into space to learn more about the solar system. Exploring space is expensive, though — the annual budget for NASA is currently $24.875 billion!

THE EUROPEAN SPACE AGENCY

In 1962, several countries in Europe decided to create two new agencies together to focus on space exploration. The European Launch Development Organization (ELDO) worked on inventing a launch system, while the European Space Research Organization (ERSO) concentrated on designing spacecraft.

The two projects remained separate until 1975 when they merged to form the European Space Agency (ESA). The ESA had 10 original founding countries: Belgium, Denmark, France, Germany, Italy, the Netherlands, Spain, Sweden, Switzerland, and the United Kingdom. Ireland joined a short time later.

The ESA now has 22 member nations with its headquarters in Paris, France. Other facilities are spread throughout Europe with multiple countries hosting different field centers. The European Space Security and Education Center is in Belgium, while ESA Mission Control is in Germany. The ESA's official languages are

English and French, but many documents are also translated into German and Italian.

ROSCOSMOS

The Soviet space program was formed in the 1950s, and it soon had the technology and knowledge to beat the United States in the early years of the Space Race. The Soviet Union set many records, including sending a human into space for the first time. However, the Soviet Union collapsed in 1991, and Russia emerged as a new country. That meant the Soviet space program needed to evolve as well.

Within a few months, the Soviet space program became the Russian Space Agency and continued its work on space exploration. The name and structure changed again in both 1999 and 2004. Finally, this space program merged with the United Rocket and Space Corporation to create the current version of Roscosmos in 2015.

THE CHINA NATIONAL SPACE ADMINISTRATION

After the United States and Russia sent astronauts into space in the 1960s, it took several decades for another country to follow. The China National Space Administration (CNSA) successfully launched the *Shenzhou-5* spacecraft in October 2003 with one person onboard, making China the third country to successfully send an astronaut into space.

In the years that followed, the CNSA focused on making its technology even better. The *Shenzhou 6* included a crew of two people, and its mission included tests to make space travel safer and more comfortable for the astronauts. The *Shenzhou 7* launched in 2008 and involved the CNSA's first spacewalk.

On December 14, 2013, the CNSA sent a lander named *Chang'e-3* to the moon. The lander was accompanied by the rover *Yutu*. While there, the rover discovered a new kind of rock and took pictures of the surface. *Yutu* continued to work until early 2015.

In the future, the CNSA hopes to send astronauts to the moon by 2030. China has also worked with Russia to come up with an idea for an International Lunar Research Station. It plans to build the station in multiple stages spread over several years.

FAMOUS SPACE MISSIONS

The public has been fascinated with space exploration ever since the first astronaut reached orbit. However, some missions are more famous than others because they set records, made a new discovery, or experienced an unexpected problem.

People are also more likely to remember the astronauts and missions from their own countries. For example, you might have heard about Neil Armstrong or the *Apollo 13* rescue before picking up this book, but you probably didn't know the name of famous astronauts from the Soviet Union. As you learn more about space exploration, remember that space agencies all over the world — not just NASA — have accomplished amazing things.

VOSTOK 1

The *Vostok 1* was the first spacecraft to carry an astronaut into space. It launched on April 12, 1961, from Baikonur, Kazakhstan as part of the Soviet Union's space program. On that day, Yuri Gagarin became the first human to ever reach orbit.

Gagarin had started his career as a pilot in the Soviet military. In 1960, the Soviet Union began a secret search to find potential astronauts, and Gagarin was chosen to become part of the "Sochi Six," the group that would fly the first Soviet missions in space.

After launch, the *Vostok 1* completed a full orbit around Earth. It took a little over an hour to complete the mission before returning to the surface. The mission was controlled from the ground, since no one was sure how going into space would affect a human being. They wanted to keep control in case Gagarin was unable to fly on his own.

PROJECT MERCURY

By the late 1950s, the U.S. military had already studied what it would take to send someone into space. Their research helped NASA establish Project Mercury and prepare for manned missions above the Earth. At last, it was time to choose the first set of U.S.

astronauts! Since seven people were selected to jumpstart the space program, the group was nicknamed the "Mercury Seven."

The members of the Mercury Seven were recruited from different branches of the military. Some of the astronauts, such as Scott Carpenter and Deke Slayton, only went into space a single time. Others broke records and continued going into space after the Mercury missions were over. Wally Schirra participated in missions for Mercury, Gemini, and Apollo before retiring on July 1, 1969. Meanwhile, Gordon Cooper spent eight days in space on *Gemini 5*.

THE APOLLO 13 CRISIS

The *Apollo 13* moon landing is one of the most famous events in history. It launched on April 11, 1970, with the goal of being the third spacecraft to land on the moon. The commander of the mission was James Lovell, NASA's most experienced astronaut. Lovell had already completed three missions, circled the moon once, and spent over 500 hours in space. The other two astronauts, Fred Haise and John "Jack" Swigert, were both going into space for the first time.

The spacecraft carrying the *Apollo 13* crew was actually made of two different vehicles. The first was named *Odyssey*, while the second was called *Aquarius*. The *Odyssey* was supposed to orbit above the moon while Lovell and Haise took the *Aquarius* to land on the surface. Unfortunately, the mission didn't exactly go as planned.

About 56 hours after launch, an oxygen tank exploded and damaged the *Odyssey*. The crew realized they wouldn't be able to complete their mission, but the *Aquarius* moon lander still had an important role to play. The *Odyssey* wasn't safe for the astronauts anymore, so the *Aquarius* became their lifeboat.

The astronauts were extremely uncomfortable in the *Aquarius* because it was only designed to fit two people, and there were three astronauts on the mission. They didn't have enough food or heat. They also needed to use some of their water to make sure the *Aquarius* didn't overheat. The conditions were so difficult that Haise started having kidney problems.

As they got closer to Earth, the crew had to go back to the *Odyssey*. The *Aquarius* lander didn't have the special shield it would need to protect the spacecraft as it entered Earth's atmosphere. The *Odyssey* made it through, and all three astronauts landed safely in the Pacific Ocean on April 17. They were picked up by a U.S. Navy ship before eventually making their way back to Houston.

CHANDRAYAAN-1

The *Chandrayaan-1* mission was the Indian Space Research Organization's first time sending a probe to the moon. It launched in late October 2008 from Sriharikota, India. On November 14, the *Chandrayaan-1* sent a Moon Impact Probe to the surface to collect samples.

Once the probe collected enough dust, the samples were analyzed by a NASA tool called the Moon Mineralogy Mapper. That's how the world discovered the moon has a form of ice on its surface.

FUTURE OF SPACE EXPLORATION

No one knows what the future holds for space exploration. After the Space Race ended in 1975, many Americans thought the country had accomplished its goals. The United States beat the Soviet Union to the moon, proving that America had an incredible team of scientists and experts at NASA.

Investing more time and money into space exploration didn't seem right at the time. Americans were focused on the Vietnam War and the economy. They thought planning more missions in space would take millions of dollars away from people who needed help from the government.

Supporters of the space program thought it was important to keep researching and exploring, but that didn't necessarily need to involve sending astronauts far away from Earth. Instead, NASA focused on the International Space Station and sending astronauts into low orbit. The agency also launched probes to study distant planets and other celestial objects.

Today, people are more open to exploring space and sending astronauts to new locations. Unfortunately, since space exploration is so expensive, it isn't possible to study everything scientists want to learn. NASA also needs to work with other countries, since many missions involve more than one space agency.

VISITING MARS IN PERSON

Astronauts won't be able to land on Mars anytime soon. NASA believes it may be possible to reach Mars by the 2030s, but it's still studying how to make such a long journey — it could take almost two years for astronauts to travel to Mars and back! The current record for the longest trip to space belongs to the Russian astronaut Valeri Polyakov, who spent 437 days onboard the *Mir* space station.

Once the astronauts arrive on Mars, they'll need specialized equipment to stay alive. NASA is testing a device that would allow the crew to produce oxygen while on Mars, and teams on the International Space Station are also working on systems to recycle food and water. They also need to figure out where the astronauts will live and work while they're on the surface.

SPACE TOURISM

Space tourism is a recent trend that started in the early 2000s. It allows people to purchase tickets on private spacecraft for short trips into space. These spaceflights are different from NASA's missions because their purpose is entertainment and provide a once-in-a-lifetime experience. Passengers aren't official astronauts, so they don't need to complete the same training as NASA personnel.

The first flight with a space tourist took place in April 2001. An American businessman named Dennis Tito traveled into space on a Russian spacecraft. He visited the International Space Station and spent just under 8 days in space. This paved the way for other companies to consider offering commercial flights to tourists.

At the time, NASA personnel criticized the idea of space tourism. However, Russia didn't feel the same way. They continued to allow tourists to take similar flights for the next eight years. A total of seven space tourists went into space during that time, and each person paid about $20 million for the experience.

Several companies now offer commercial space flights. SpaceX, Virgin Galactic, and Blue Origin are the most famous. However, space tourism is only a small part of their businesses—they also collaborate with the government and other organizations to support space exploration.

FINDING HABITABLE PLANETS

There are so many planets in the universe that it's impossible to know whether any others can support human life. Some planets are too far away to study, even with probes capable of traveling billions of miles. Finding a habitable planet isn't just a matter of discovering water, though; a planet also needs to have enough oxygen to breathe and surface temperatures that humans can survive.

Researchers are interested in finding a habitable planet because it could serve as a launch point for future missions. It would allow a spacecraft to stop on a long journey for supplies and maintenance. NASA has even considered whether building a base on the moon would help astronauts reach Mars.

SOLVING MYSTERIES

In the future, exploring different parts of the galaxy may help astronomers solve mysteries about what's really "out there." For example, some scientists believe there's another planet at the far edge of our solar system. For now, it's nicknamed "Planet Nine," since no one knows for sure whether it actually exists.

Astronomers came up with the idea of Planet Nine when they were studying how comets and asteroids move in the Kuiper Belt. Other objects in the area acted like there was another planet nearby. If Planet Nine is real, it would be about the same size as Neptune and take up to 20,000 years to complete a full orbit around the sun.

IMPROVING SAFETY

Unfortunately, space exploration is dangerous, even with the best planning. There have been multiple accidents throughout history where astronauts lost their lives from mistakes, miscalculations, or broken equipment. We've already mentioned one of these, but some incidents have also occurred after launch.

On January 28, 1986, the seven astronauts onboard the space shuttle *Challenger* were killed when the spacecraft broke up 73 seconds after liftoff. Investigators later discovered that some of the rubber used to build the rocket booster failed because of low temperatures. In fact, the temperature in Cape Canaveral, Florida was so low on January 28 that it broke the record for the lowest temperature ever recorded in that area.

The *Challenger* accident taught NASA about the importance of making sure equipment was used the way it was tested. If something wasn't tested in extremely cold temperatures, then it would be risky to use it in extremely cold temperatures. The loss of the *Challenger* crew also revealed problems with how NASA employees worked together and talked about safety. NASA realized it needed to be more careful about how it treated risks.

However, NASA continued to struggle with schedules, budgets, and safety reviews. On February 1, 2003, the space shuttle *Columbia* fell apart while reentering the atmosphere. The cause was a piece of foam that had broken off during takeoff. Engineers knew about the foam, but they didn't think it was capable of causing any damage to the shuttle.

In reality, the foam had hit the left wing and created a tear. When the spacecraft attempted its return to Earth, hot air made its way into the hole. The accident might have been prevented if someone had suggested using a satellite to examine the spacecraft. NASA could also have approved a spacewalk so the astronauts could check the wing.

The public and the U.S. government were critical of NASA's safety choices, and many people doubted whether it was worth it to continue exploring space. Now that the space program is becoming popular again, it's important to learn from past mistakes. Even though it's upsetting to read about these events, studying what happened is the only way to keep astronauts safe for future missions.

CONTRIBUTIONS OF SPACE EXPLORATION

Space exploration has resulted in all types of new gadgets, devices, and inventions. Since many ordinary objects could break down in space, NASA and other space agencies have needed to redesign different tools and household items. Their inventions often lasted longer or did a better job than older designs, so they've slowly made their way into regular society.

Space exploration's contributions to society don't stop there. Exploring the universe has united people from different countries, cultures, and backgrounds. From watching the moon landing to multiple space agencies working together on the International Space Station, space exploration helps the world come together as a single planet.

SMALL SATELLITES

Small satellites are making it easier to study Earth and learn more about our own planet. In fact, some of the satellites NASA has sent into space are as small as a loaf of bread! That makes it cheaper and easier to collect information without cluttering the area around Earth. NASA and its partners use these satellites to measure hurricanes, protect animal habitats, and track climate change.

SAFETY EQUIPMENT

Since space travel is so dangerous, NASA needs all types of unusual safety equipment to protect astronauts. Some of these items are so brilliant that they've made their way to the general public and emergency response agencies.

One of NASA's simplest inventions is the foil blanket that's jokingly called a "space blanket." These sheets are used to hold in heat and protect astronauts from getting too cold as they traveled through space. Nowadays, they're often included in first aid kits, in case anyone gets overexposed to the cold.

NASA is also responsible for designing the rescue tool that's best known as the "Jaws of Life." Firefighters and other first responders use the Jaws of Life to cut into cars after an accident, though NASA used a much larger version to separate rocket boosters and space shuttles.

You can even credit NASA scientists with making swimming pools safer. During the 1960s, NASA came up with a new way to purify water in space, and the same technique is now used to kill bacteria in pools.

CAMERA PHONES

Camera phones are common household objects, but it wasn't always easy to create cameras of that size. NASA needed smaller cameras that could fit on a spacecraft without taking up too much room. The camera also had to be capable of taking detailed pictures for scientific research. The Jet Propulsion Laboratory in California invented a camera in the 1990s that matched those requirements, and roughly one out of every three cameras still use the same technology.

MEMORY FOAM

You might be able to find one of NASA's most famous inventions right inside your mattress! In 1966, NASA created a special type of foam that would protect astronauts and pilots during flight. Before long, people started to wonder whether the foam could be used for other things that need cushions. That's how "memory foam" eventually appeared in couches and beds. The Dallas Cowboys even used it inside their helmets during the 1970s and 1980s.

Interestingly, NASA found a new way to use memory foam in the early 2000s. They used the foam to build a squishy floor that would put people off balance as they walked across it. When astronauts returned to Earth and needed to regain their sense of balance, NASA challenged them with the foam floor.

FREEZE-DRIED FOOD

When NASA was planning the Apollo missions, it looked into different ways to keep food from going bad. The astronauts needed nutritious food, but they couldn't carry anything too heavy or difficult to store. NASA eventually invented the process of freeze-drying, which removes moisture from food. This makes food up to 80 percent lighter, without losing any of the vitamins or nutrients.

A company named Action Products used the same technique to create foods such as freeze-dried ice cream. At first, these freeze-dried desserts were sold to the public as an interesting new treat. However, people soon realized freeze-drying food could be helpful in other situations besides going to space, and freeze-dried meals are now used for camping, emergency rations, and traveling in areas without easy access to other foods.

INTERNATIONAL COOPERATION

Space exploration has led to amazing discoveries, gadgets, and devices. However, one of its most amazing achievements is uniting people from all over the world. In modern times, space agencies from different countries frequently work together on shared projects like the International Space Station.

During the Space Race and the Cold War, political tensions were high between the United States and the Soviet Union, and space exploration gave both countries something in common. Astronauts from both countries even shook hands in space on July 17, 1975, to show that they could put aside their differences while working together on a shared project.

CHAPTER FOUR:
SPACE PHENOMENA
AND MYSTERIES

Space is full of mysteries and unusual phenomena that can seem almost magical when viewed from Earth. Phenomena like eclipses are well understood by scientists, but some events are still hard to explain, even with all of today's technology. It could be hundreds or thousands of years before astronomers have the tools they need to fully study certain ideas.

Luckily, scientists know that it's okay to make mistakes or come up with theories that don't work out in the end. The earliest astronomers didn't even know that the sun was the center of solar system! As space agencies make new discoveries and send probes farther into space, we'll slowly learn more and more about the galaxy we all call home.

ECLIPSES

Solar eclipses occur when the moon is in between the Earth and the sun. From Earth, it appears like the sun is going dark. Partial solar eclipses usually take place a few times per year. A total solar eclipse (when the sun is completely covered) only happens about once every 18 months.

Lunar eclipses, on the other hand, occur when the Earth is in between the moon and the sun. The shadow from Earth makes the moon's surface look dark. Total lunar eclipses take place about every two and a half years.

FAMOUS ECLIPSES

Even though eclipses are common, there have still been some famous eclipses throughout history. Here are just a few of the most important eclipses:

- In the year 418 CE, a historian named Philostorgius sketched an eclipse which included a comet in the sky. It was the first time anyone had ever reported seeing a comet and an eclipse at the same time.

- Hundreds of years later, in 1836, the English astronomer Francis Baily figured out why some small beads of light seem to shine around the edges of solar eclipses. This was when Baily realized the moon's surface wasn't completely smooth, so light was able to shine around high points and craters.

- In July 1851, the Russian photographer Julius Berkowski took the first picture of a total eclipse. He used a 2.4-inch telescope and snapped the picture from Königsberg, Prussia.

If you want to see an eclipse for yourself, visit NASA's website! They maintain a list of upcoming solar and lunar eclipses that you can check out.

SAFETY DURING SOLAR ECLIPSES

Solar eclipses are fascinating, but they can also be dangerous without the right safety equipment. Looking directly at a solar eclipse can damage your eyes unless you're wearing eclipse glasses. Eclipse glasses are much darker than other types of lenses or sunglasses. It's not even safe to view a solar eclipse through telescopes or cameras.

METEOR SHOWERS

Meteor showers occur when pieces of rock or metal fall from space and enter Earth's atmosphere. Most of these objects burn up, producing streaks of light. If you've ever wished on a shooting star, you were actually looking at a meteor.

Most of the objects that fall to Earth broke free from comets or asteroids. When Earth comes close to a comet or asteroid, pieces get pulled into Earth's gravity. Since comets and the planets move on consistent paths, it's possible to see the same meteor shower from one year to the next. The Perseid meteor shower usually happens between the middle of July and the end of August.

NORTHERN LIGHTS
AND OTHER ATMOSPHERIC
PHENOMENA

Atmospheric phenomena are fascinating because they create such beautiful patterns in the sky. However, though they might seem magical, there's a scientific explanation for why rainbows, light pillars, and other phenomena form.

THE NORTHERN LIGHTS

The northern lights are famous around the world for making vivid colors and patterns in the sky. These displays occur when explosions on the sun's surface cause particles to hit Earth's atmosphere. The magnetic field around Earth protects the planet from harm, but some of those particles interact with gases around the north and south poles. That's why you don't see these types of lights in most parts of the world.

Before scientists understood what was happening on the sun's surface, many people thought the northern lights were caused by supernatural forces. The ancient Greeks and Romans believed the northern lights were made by the Goddess of the Dawn. In China, people thought they were two dragons fighting over good and evil.

LIGHT PILLARS

Light pillars look like giant beams of light shooting up from the ground to the sky. These pillars form when there are ice crystals in the atmosphere. Since the crystals are flat, they reflect light back down to Earth's surface. Light pillars are most often seen in cold environments during the winter, and some even appear to be different colors.

WHITE RAINBOWS AND DEWBOWS

You've probably seen a rainbow appear after a rainstorm. Ordinary rainbows show all colors, appearing when light passes through drops of water. However, there are also white rainbows that appear in fog and smaller droplets. White rainbows don't have the same range of colors, but they may sometimes have a blue or red edge.

Dewbows are created in a similar way, when light passes through dew. They tend to be smaller and can form on grass, spider webs, or other outdoor objects. Unlike traditional rainbows or white bows, dewbows make a complete circle instead of just an arch.

NACREOUS CLOUDS

Nacreous clouds are also known as *ice polar stratospheric clouds*. The clouds contain tiny bits of ice that reflect the light around them. Nacreous clouds are usually only seen in places like Scotland and Alaska that have extremely cold temperatures and mountains. It's rare to see nacreous clouds because the atmosphere needs to be negative 121 degrees Fahrenheit.

UNEXPLAINED MYSTERIES

Dark matter and dark energy are extremely complicated to understand. Scientists throughout history have wondered whether some parts of the universe might be invisible. The idea gained momentum as technology allowed astronomers to see farther away from Earth, and most scientists now agree that some form of dark matter and dark energy exist.

DARK MATTER

Normal objects are made up of matter, which means they have weight and take up space. Even the air around us contains matter! *Dark* matter is different because it doesn't reflect or give off any light. The idea has caused many people to ask how it's possible to prove that something exists if you can't see it.

Scientists as far back as the 1920s have looked at the sky for answers. The way stars move makes it seem like there's more mass that just isn't visible to any known equipment. Astronomers also point out that galaxies need a certain amount of mass to hold themselves together. Dark matter could be the glue in between.

DARK ENERGY

The universe isn't finished growing. However, if only visible objects like planets and stars are out there in space, the universe shouldn't be expanding as fast as it is. That makes it likely that there's some other type of energy at work. Scientists believe dark energy could make up 68 percent of the entire universe.

Although dark energy isn't fully understood, space agencies hope to learn more soon. The European Space agency launched the *Euclid* telescope on July 1, 2023. Its goal is to study dark energy and dark matter from almost a million miles away from Earth.

THEORIES OF THE UNIVERSE

There's no single proven theory that describes how the universe began. Different theories have formed because there are so many things that have yet to be discovered about the universe. Without knowing all the facts, it's tough to prove that any single idea is correct. For now, the theory that's accepted by most scientists is the "Big Bang."

THE BIG BANG

According to the Big Bang Theory, the universe was stuck in a tiny bubble about 14 billion years ago. Suddenly, it exploded and grew, in a massive expansion that lasted only part of a second. From there, it kept growing until it created everything in existence today. The Big Bang Theory would explain why the universe is still expanding.

The Big Bang Theory was first developed by a Belgian priest named Georges Lemaître. Aside from his religious studies, he was also a mathematician and astronomer. At first, Lemaître's ideas centered around the theory that the universe could still be growing. His work made even more sense after 1929, when the American astronomer Edwin Hubble confirmed that the universe was expanding. Lemaître wrote a paper about the Big Bang Theory and published it in 1931.

At first, other experts were confused or simply said his theory was wrong. After all, Lemaître's ideas were very different from what other scientists believed at the time. In the 1930s, astronomers still thought the universe stayed the same and wasn't shrinking or growing. Instead, most people accepted that the universe was infinite and had simply always existed in the same way.

It took 40 years for most experts to accept the theory, but everyone agreed there needed to be more research to know for sure. Inventions like the Hubble Space Telescope and advanced satellites made it easier to prove that the universe was much different in the past. Experts hope that research into the origins of the universe will eventually help them understand other complicated issues like dark matter and dark energy.

THE BIG BOUNCE

Some researchers think the universe will eventually stop growing and shrink back on itself. Once it becomes small, it can then expand again in another big bang. This would create a cycle of growing and shrinking over billions of years. Even though most experts don't support this theory, it's obvious from the history of astronomy that people have been wrong in the past. It's possible that scientists in the future will create a new version of the Big Bang Theory as they make new discoveries.

CHAPTER FIVE:
SPACE TECHNOLOGY
AND INNOVATIONS

Space exploration has inspired scientists to create some of the most advanced equipment in the world. Traveling into space is so unpredictable and dangerous that space agencies need the best technology, gear, and materials. Every object NASA sends into space is carefully tested to make sure it works and that it's safe for astronauts to use.

NASA's inventions are designed in special labs all over the country. Here are just a few of NASA's research facilities:

- The Jet Propulsion Laboratory is located in Pasadena, California. It specializes in building space probes, satellites, and Mars rovers.

- The NASA Safety Center in Cleveland, Ohio, develops tools and processes to keep NASA personnel safe during missions.

- The Neil Armstrong Test Facility in Sandusky, Ohio, has training simulators for astronauts and specialized methods of testing equipment. It even has a hypersonic wind tunnel, which can reach speeds of up to Mach 7!

Experts at each NASA facility work together to support different areas of space exploration. They also share information with other space agencies and collaborate on shared projects. For example, the European Space Agency and NASA worked together at the Jet Propulsion Laboratory to launch the *Ulysses* space probe in 1990.

HOW ROCKETS WORK

A rocket is responsible for helping an object like a spacecraft or a missile take off from the ground. Scientifically, they're known as *propulsion devices*. If you've ever seen someone launch fireworks, you should already have an idea of how rockets work. Basically, rockets burn fuel and turn it into hot gas. The gas is propelled out of the back of the rocket, which gives it enough force to send the rocket and another object up into space.

Rocket engines are different from other types of engines used on Earth. There's no oxygen in space, so engines need to be able to work without air. These types of engines help spacecraft like the International Space Station stay in the right place — otherwise, Earth's gravity will continue to pull on the station and cause it to fall back to the surface. That's why the ordinary engines used in airplanes can't function outside Earth's atmosphere.

ROCKET FUEL

Rockets can either run on solid or liquid fuel. Solid fuels are cheaper, but they aren't as easy to control. Engines that use liquid fuel can also be stopped and restarted. NASA uses both at different times, depending on the mission.

The rockets involved in space exploration have more than one part, or "stage." When all the fuel has been used up in one stage, it separates from the rest of the spacecraft to get rid of the extra weight. Then, the pieces fall back to Earth, while the rest of the launcher continues into space. The two solid rocket boosters on space shuttles use 11,000 pounds of fuel per second!

SPACE TELESCOPES

Unlike telescopes that we use on the surface, space telescopes are launched into space to give scientists an even closer look at the universe. Since Earth's atmosphere blocks light and has pockets of air that move, pictures taken from the ground still appear blurry, even if they're taken with advanced telescopes. Because of this, NASA decided to launch telescopes directly into space.

THE FIRST SPACE TELESCOPE

Though it's not the most famous, the first telescope in space was the Orbiting Astronomical Observatory 2, or OAO 2 for short. It launched on December 7, 1968, just a few weeks before *Apollo 8* proved that it was possible to reach the moon.

OAO 2 was able to take thousands of measurements of the universe, without having to worry about interference from Earth's atmosphere. This data showed that young stars were even hotter than scientists believed at the time. The telescope was also able to confirm that comets are surrounded by hydrogen clouds.

Launching OAO 2 also taught NASA how to operate a telescope in space. It was difficult to keep the telescope pointed at one object, but that was an important part of studying distant places and objects. These challenges helped NASA figure out what to improve when they designed another telescope in the future.

THE HUBBLE SPACE TELESCOPE

The Hubble Space Telescope was launched on April 24, 1990. In total, it took $1.5 billion to design. The telescope stays in orbit 340 miles above Earth, traveling about 17,000 miles per hour. At that speed, it takes the Hubble 95 minutes to complete a full orbit.

The telescope was named after the American astronomer Edwin P. Hubble. During the early 1900s, he realized that our solar system and galaxy only make up one small part of the whole universe. His discoveries helped other scientists understand how the universe formed billions of years ago.

The Hubble has a guiding system that can lock onto targets throughout the universe. The farthest it's managed to look is at galaxy GN-z11, which is 13.4 billion light-years away from Earth! The telescope uses specialized lights and sensors to study different objects. For example, the Cosmic Origins Spectrograph aboard the Hubble studies ultraviolet light and how stars, planets, and galaxies form.

No one knows exactly how long the Hubble Space Telescope will last. It turned 30 years old in 2020 and could last until 2040. Since it uses solar power from the sun, it doesn't run out of fuel or energy. When Hubble reaches the end of its life, research will continue with newer, more-advanced space telescopes.

THE JAMES WEBB SPACE TELESCOPE

The James Webb Space Telescope is even more powerful than the Hubble Space Telescope. It was designed to fold up for launch, but it's actually as tall as a three-story building. The telescope cost $10 billion to make, and it launched into space on Christmas Day in 2021.

The James Webb Space Telescope was originally named the Next Generation Space Telescope. In 2002, it was renamed in honor of NASA's administrator from 1961 to 1968. James E. Webb led NASA through a major part of its history and oversaw the Mercury and Gemini missions.

Unlike the Hubble, the James Webb Space Telescope traveled deeper into space to be able to see distant areas. It stopped a million miles away, in between Earth and Mars. The telescope is able to study clouds of dust where new planets are forming and learn more about the planets that orbit other stars.

NANCY GRACE ROMAN SPACE TELESCOPE

The Nancy Grace Roman Space Telescope is scheduled to launch in 2027, after completing testing at the Goddard Space Flight Center. It will travel away from Earth and end up close to the James Webb Space Telescope. This telescope is expected to be in use for at least five years.

The telescope was named after NASA's first chief of astronomy. After starting at NASA in 1959, Nancy Roman was responsible for accepting or rejecting new projects at NASA. She also played an important role in creating the Hubble Space Telescope. She believed placing a telescope in orbit above the Earth made more sense than trying to put one on the moon where dust would be a problem.

The Nancy Grace Roman Space Telescope will study exoplanets outside our solar system and help scientists learn more about dark matter. The updated design will give it a view that's 100 times wider than what the Hubble can currently see.

SPACE STATIONS

The International Space Station is one of only two space stations ever created. It was built by five different space agencies: NASA, Roscosmos, the Japan Aerospace Exploration Agency, the Canadian Space Agency, and the European Space Agency. NASA spends more than $3 billion every year maintaining it.

Over 250 people from 21 different countries have visited the International Space Station since construction started in 1998. Most astronauts on the ISS stay for about six months. Since the station was only designed to host a crew of six astronauts at a time, not every country that participates can have an astronaut on the station at the same time.

The International Space Station won't last forever—it's only scheduled to last until 2030. NASA plans to eventually build a replacement and let the current ISS crash into the ocean. Building a new space station will allow NASA and other space agencies to take advantage of new technologies and discoveries.

Besides the International Space Station, there's also the Tiangong, which belongs to China. The first section was launched on April 28, 2021, and a crew from the Chinese Manned Space Agency arrived a short time later, on June 16. The Tiangong space station is smaller than the ISS, so it only has a crew of three astronauts at a time.

Taking care of the Tiangong is challenging for China because it doesn't have any partners from around the world. For political reasons, NASA isn't allowed to work with China, even on the International Space Station. That's why China had to build its own space station.

SLEEPING IN SPACE

Sleeping in space is difficult because of how light changes from one hour to the next. Unlike a 24-hour day on Earth, astronauts only get 45 minutes of daylight at a time before it gets dark again. During a single orbit, there will be 16 sunrises and 16 sunsets. That makes it a lot harder for astronauts to stay on a healthy schedule.

Since astronauts also have to learn how to sleep without gravity, NASA invented its own sleeping position to help crew members reduce stress on their bodies in space. It involves lifting their heads and legs slightly above their hearts while they're asleep. Astronauts sleep in special sleeping bags that are tied to a wall.

The ISS only has six sleeping cabins, so crews sometimes need to get creative when there are more than six people on the station at a time. Astronauts on the Tiangong don't need to worry about that, though, since they have room for three additional people.

EATING AND DRINKING

Eating on space stations is a lot easier than it used to be. In the past, astronauts had to eat food paste out of tubes. As you can imagine, that wasn't the most exciting way to eat! Nowadays, astronauts eat regular food out of special containers. Drinks are all powdered, so crew members need to add water first.

To keep their food from floating away, astronauts connect their trays to either the wall or their laps. Food containers stick to the tray, but crew members still eat with regular utensils.

WORKING OUT AND EXERCISE EQUIPMENT

Because astronauts lose muscle and bone mass while in space, they need to exercise for at least two hours every day to stay healthy. Working out is especially hard in space because of differences in gravity. Ordinary weights, for example, won't work in low gravity.

The International Space Station has a gym, with a treadmill, a bicycle, and a special weightlifting machine known as the Advanced Resistive Exercise Device. On the Tiangong space station, there are multiple fitness areas with exercise equipment.

DANGERS AND RISKS

Astronauts who work on space stations keep in touch with personnel on the surface to stay safe. Though there are always people checking on the astronauts, there are still some problems that catch the world's space agencies by surprise.

In November 2021, NASA had to wake up the astronauts on the ISS to tell them about space debris in the area. The debris was caused when Russia destroyed one of its satellites. The astronauts didn't have enough time to move away from the objects, so NASA told them to evacuate the space station until they were sure none of the debris would crash into it. The seven astronauts waited in their spacecraft in case they had to abandon the station.

Tiangong had a similar problem in March 2024, when debris damaged the station's solar panels. The crew had to go outside to make repairs. It was the first time Chinese astronauts had ever made spacewalks, but they were able to fix the panels and make it back inside.

The threat posed by space debris could become a bigger issue in the future. As more satellites enter orbit, more materials could hit space stations or other important equipment. Scientists are still figuring out the best way to get rid of items in space once they're no longer needed.

ROBOTICS IN SPACE

Robots have played an important role in learning more about the universe. Space agencies use robots to explore distant or dangerous areas where it wouldn't be possible to send human astronauts. These devices allow us to study the surfaces of moons and other planets using cameras, sensors, and other specialized equipment.

The robots used in space exploration come in three main categories:

- *Orbiters* stay above the surface of planets, moons, or other celestial objects.

- *Landers* stay in one place once they're on the surface.

- *Rovers* can move around the surface.

NASA uses all three types of robots, depending on what it wants to study. An orbiter is usually sent ahead of time to find good landing locations for a lander and rover. NASA's Mars Reconnaissance Orbiter has been in place above Mars since 2006.

LUNAR ROVERS

Unlike the robotic rovers used on Mars, lunar rovers are used by astronauts while on the surface. The vehicles are nicknamed "moon buggies." The first lunar roving vehicle, or LRV, was built in 1969. It launched in 1971 on *Apollo 15*, and astronauts David

Scott and James Irwin drove it on the moon's surface. During the mission, the astronauts used a Lunar Roving Vehicle to find samples. Having a rover allowed them to spend longer on the surface of the moon and collect more samples than two other missions combined.

The LRV worked so well for *Apollo 15* that the next two missions to the moon took a rover with them, too. The astronauts used the LRV to travel farther than they could on foot. The rover used for *Apollo 16* and *Apollo 17* could drive up to 10 miles per hour.

NASA plans to use rovers again when *Artemis 3* lands on the moon in 2026. The agency is also working on upgraded devices known as *lunar terrain vehicles*. The new rovers won't be ready in time for *Artemis 3*, so NASA hopes to launch them with the crew of *Artemis 5* in 2030. The goal is to invent self-driving rovers that can travel for up to eight hours per day.

Even with these new designs, NASA is always looking for ways to improve their lunar rovers. Every year, NASA sponsors the Human Exploration Rover Challenge, an engineering competition that lets students in high school and college design rovers for use on the moon. The competition first started in 1995. It takes place every year in Huntsville, Alabama, at the U.S. Space & Rocket Center. Students test their rover designs on a track that includes obstacles like gravel and bumps.

MARS ROVERS

During the 1990s, NASA was especially interested in learning about Mars. It designed a mission to send a robotic lander with an attached rover to the surface. *Pathfinder* and its rover *Sojourner* launched from Florida on December 4, 1996. It took over half a year to reach Mars and attempt to land in early July.

Pathfinder used an unusual method to reach the surface. Instead of trying to land perfectly, it used parachutes to slow down, then deployed giant airbags to avoid getting damaged. It was the first time any mission had used that kind of technology, but it worked! *Pathfinder* and *Sojourner* became the first robots to land on the Red Planet.

Both robots had special tools and equipment to study Mars. *Pathfinder* spent more than two years collecting information from the surface. It sent back over 16,500 pictures and analyzed the rocks, soil, and weather. The data from *Pathfinder* and *Sojourner* showed that Mars might have been warmer and had water in the past.

Spirit and *Opportunity* were the next to reach Mars in January 2004. Their mission was to search the surface for clues about the environment and whether Mars might have been able to support life in the past. Even though the rovers were only designed for a 90-day mission, they both lasted far longer than expected. *Spirit* made it all the way to March 2010, and *Opportunity* lasted until February 2019.

Curiosity launched in late 2011 and arrived on August 6, 2012. Its mission was to find out whether Mars was ever able to support microbial life. Microbes include tiny life-forms, like bacteria. *Curiosity* has 17 different cameras and a 7-foot arm that makes it easier for the rover to pick up rocks and collect samples.

After the launch of *Curiosity*, NASA took a long break before sending another rover to Mars. The China National Space Administration launched *Zhurong* on July 22, 2020, making it the second country to land a rover on another planet. *Zhurong* studied the surface of Mars until May 20, 2022, when it went into hibernation during the winter. It was supposed to wake up later, but there was too much dust for it to work.

NASA's most recent rover, *Perseverance*, launched only eight days after *Zhurong* to collect samples of soil and rock from the surface. *Perseverance* landed in Jezero Crater, where scientists think there might have once been a lake. If life ever existed on Mars, Jezero Crater is high on the list of possible locations.

NASA and the European Space Agency are working together on a mission to bring samples collected by *Perseverance* back to Earth. This would involve sending a robot to land on Mars and launch the samples back to an orbiter. The mission is complicated and hard to plan and has an estimated cost of up to $11 billion.

FUTURE
TECHNOLOGIES

From movies to science fiction novels, there are plenty of stories that involve technologies from the future. Some characters hop from one galaxy to the next with just the push of a button, while others track down their alternate selves in parallel universes. These ideas don't always make sense in terms of real science, but some aren't as impossible as you might think.

LONG-DISTANCE COMMUNICATION

Being able to send and receive long-distance messages is important for keeping in touch with spacecraft. Because of how the Earth rotates, it isn't possible to use just one antenna, so NASA has three giant radio antennas around the world that make up the Deep Space Network. The network is operated by the Jet Propulsion Laboratory.

The three antennas are located on the West Coast of the United States, the middle of Spain, and southeastern Australia. These areas were chosen because they allow NASA to keep in constant communication with spacecraft. Each antenna has a dish that's 230 feet across. The antennas can track a spacecraft for billions of miles. That's how NASA has managed to stay in contact with *Voyager 1*, even though it's over 15 billion miles away from Earth.

American astronomer Howard Isaacson wonders whether long-distance signals from the Deep Space Network might be the key to finding alien life. When signals reach spacecraft like *Voyager 1*, they don't end there — they continue deeper into space, where they could be picked up by other planets. Isaacson believes the closest planets would have enough time to receive a message and reply by the year 2031.

WARP DRIVES AND INTERSTELLAR TRAVEL

In science fiction, travelers can often jump from one location to another using special drives. While it's unlikely that we'll ever figure out interstellar travel, there is one way extremely distant spaces could be connected: wormholes.

Some scientists believe wormholes could exist, based on what we know about gravity. In 1935, Albert Einstein and the American-Israeli physicist Nathan Rosen came up with the idea that black holes and other areas with strong gravity might be able to connect. That would create a type of bridge between two different areas of the universe that we call a wormhole.

ENERGY SHIELDS

Energy shields appear in many science fiction stories to protect spacecraft during battles or while flying around debris. This technology doesn't exist in real life, but that doesn't mean NASA hasn't thought about it.

In 2005, NASA researchers came up with a way to use an electric field and specially designed spheres to protect against radiation. A year later, scientists at the University of Washington experimented with plasma and mesh to see if they could invent a shield for spacecraft. Neither of these ideas were successful, but they proved that NASA isn't afraid to experiment with unusual ideas.

CHAPTER SIX: SPACE FACTS AND RECORDS

Looking at facts and records from space will give you an idea of just how different Earth is from the rest of the universe. It might seem like our planet is full of diversity when you think of the difference between Antarctica and the desert, but space has even bigger extremes.

The records set by some of the most unusual places and objects in space will probably be broken in the future. So far, we've only explored a tiny piece of the universe. As scientists figure out how to go even farther and see even deeper into space, we're almost guaranteed to make new record-breaking discoveries.

LARGEST, SMALLEST, HOTTEST, AND COLDEST

Space is full of dangerous places that could destroy probes or robotics in just a few seconds. Since it's not always possible to send a spacecraft, space agencies study these areas using space telescopes or by flying nearby at a safe distance. In the future, we might be able to learn more if we can develop robots and spacecraft out of stronger materials.

THE BIGGEST VOIDS IN THE UNIVERSE

When an area of space doesn't have as many galaxies as it should, it's known as a *void* or *supervoid*. The Böotes Void was one of the first ones found. It was discovered in 1981 by American astronomer Robert Kirshner. At almost 330 million light-years wide, it held the record as the largest void for many years.

The current record for the largest void is held by LOWZ North 13788, which is nearly three billion light-years wide and contains over 109,000 known galaxies. The void that's considered second place is still being investigated. The KBC Void is 2 million light-years across. This void is especially interesting because it contains our galaxy.

THE BIGGEST AND SMALLEST STARS

The sun in our solar system is in the top 12 percent of all stars in the universe. The award for the biggest star goes to UY Scuti. It's located about 6,000 light-years away from Earth, and you can only see it with a telescope. UY Scuti is so large that it could fit our sun inside of it five *billion* times! If UY Scuti replaced our sun, its outer edge would reach past Jupiter.

The record for the smallest star belongs to EBLM J0555-57Ab. This tiny star was discovered in 2017 by researchers in England. It's located about 600 light-years away in the same galaxy as Earth. Scientists don't think stars can get much smaller than EBLM J0555-57Ab because of the processes that allows it to become a star in the first place. Even though EBLM J0555-57Ab is small for a star, it's about the same size as Saturn.

THE UNIVERSE'S HOTTEST AND COLDEST PLACES

The hottest place in the universe is a supermassive black hole called quasar 3C273. The black hole is about 2.4 billion light-years away from Earth. Astronomers at the Greenbank Observatory in West Virginia believe that it gets as hot as 18 *trillion* degrees Fahrenheit in the plasma around the black hole!

On the other end of the scale, the coldest place in the universe is the Boomerang Nebula at almost negative 460 degrees Fahrenheit. It's located about 5,000 light-years away, and the dying star inside the nebula has been losing its outer layers 100 billion times faster than the sun in our solar system, pushing heat away from the area.

FASTEST AND SLOWEST

When you think about the speed of objects in space, it's only fair to separate natural objects from those made by humans. After all, even the fastest spacecraft can't compete with planets and stars! Human-made objects are limited by fuel and the materials we have available, and spacecraft are more sensitive to damage because they carry delicate equipment and, in some cases, people.

THE SPEED OF LIGHT

Technically, light is the fastest thing in existence. It moves at a speed of 186,000 miles per second, so fast that it could go around the Earth seven and a half times in a single second! The laws of physics say that the only way an object can ever reach light speed is if it has unlimited energy. Since that's not possible, light takes first place as the fastest thing in the universe.

THE FASTEST STARS IN THE MILKY WAY

In 2023, astronomers discovered six of the fastest stars ever found, and two stood out as faster than the previous record. The fastest star, called J0927, travels at a speed of 5.1 million miles per hour. The second, J1235, made it up to 3.8 million miles per hour. Both stars travel quickly enough to escape the gravity in our galaxy. The team that found the stars has a theory that they were launched to such high speeds by the explosion of another star.

SPACECRAFT AT SPEED

The fastest spacecraft, the Parker Solar Probe, keeps breaking its own record. It was launched in 2018 to study the sun and learn more about solar wind. In 2021, it reached a speed of 364,660 miles per hour, setting a new record as the fastest human-made object. On September 27, 2023, the probe increased its record to 394,736 miles per hour.

The Parker Solar Probe also holds the record for human-made objects flying closest to the sun. When it broke its own speed record in 2023, it came within 4.51 million miles of the sun's surface. NASA estimates that it will eventually get as close as 3.9 million miles away.

Choosing the slowest spacecraft is a bit of challenge since some, like the International Space Station, aren't designed to move out of orbit. The *Dawn* space probe, however, deserves some recognition. The probe was launched on September 27, 2007, with the goal of studying the asteroid Vesta and the dwarf planet Ceres.

While this sounds simple, NASA was faced with the challenge of making sure the probe had enough fuel for its journey. *Dawn* needed to travel 100 million miles just to reach its first stop at Vesta. Experts at NASA decided to use a lighter fuel that would last longer with the right travel path.

After breaking free of Earth's orbit, *Dawn* was moving so slowly that it took four days to reach 60 miles per hour, but it eventually increased speed as it moved farther away from Earth. The probe successfully reached Vesta on July 16, 2011, almost four years after departure.

LONGEST AND SHORTEST

Like the other records we've mentioned, many records in this category depend on the situation. For example, Mercury has the fastest orbit of any planet in our solar system, but it's slow compared to planets that orbit stars other than our sun. Scientists are also limited by how far they can see, so the current records probably wouldn't hold up if you could compare them to everything in the universe.

LONGEST AND SHORTEST ORBITS

The planet with the longest orbit was discovered in 2021. It was given the slightly silly name of "COCONUTS-2 b" because it was found as part of the Cool Companions on Ultrawide Orbits (Coconuts) survey. COCONUTS-2 b is a gas giant with over six times as much mass as Jupiter and takes more than 1.1 million years to finish a single orbit around its star!

The planet with the shortest orbit is TOI-2109 b. It completes a full orbit in only 16 hours. TOI-2019 b is a gas giant about five times bigger than Jupiter, but it's only 1.5 million miles away from its star. In our solar system, Mercury is over 42 million miles from the sun.

RECORDS IN ROTATION

A planet called Beta Pictoris b rotates so quickly that a day only lasts eight hours—its equator moves at a speed of 62,000 miles per hour! Earth's equator only travels at a speed of 1,060 miles per hour. Beta Pictoris b might spin even faster as it ages. It's still a young planet, so its speed of rotation will change as it ages and cools down.

In 2018, a student at the Jodrell Bank Centre for Astrophysics in England discovered a pulsar star that was rotating slower than any other ever found. Pulsar stars are made when another star explodes, so they're known for spinning at high speeds, but this one was only spinning once every 23.5 seconds. Meanwhile, the fastest pulsar star rotates 716 times per second!

HEAVIEST AND LIGHTEST

Weight and mass are two different scientific measurements. The term *weight* describes the force of gravity on an object. The amount of gravity changes from one place to the next, so you wouldn't weigh the same on Earth and on the International Space Station. Mass is how much matter is in an object, and that always stays the same.

MOST AND LEAST AMOUNT OF MASS

If you think back to what you've already learned about dark matter, you'll remember that it doesn't emit any light or energy. That makes it harder to detect, but scientists currently believe dark matter makes up 80% of all the mass in the universe. Therefore, though it isn't a single object, it's considered the category with the most mass.

In our solar system, the object with the most mass is the sun, which contains over 99.8% of all mass in the solar system. The rest of the planets, moons, comets, asteroids, and other objects in space make up the other 0.02%. Out of the planets, Jupiter has more mass than any other planet in our solar system.

The objects with the least amount of mass are tough to rank, since the record should technically belong to tiny particles out in space. Instead, it's easier to look at the lowest amount of mass for a particular type of object, planet, or star.

For example, the black hole with the least amount of mass was discovered in 2019. Up until that point, all the black holes ever found throughout the galaxy had masses that were 5 to 15 times greater than the mass of the sun. At that point, astronomers started to wonder if they could find black holes that were even smaller.

Finally, scientists found a giant red star orbiting around a black hole with a mass that was only 3.3 times that of our sun. Their work resulted in an entirely new category of low-mass black holes and proved the astronomers' theory correct. This example shows how we are constantly making new discoveries about the universe as technology advances.

HIGHEST AND LOWEST GRAVITY

Out of all the planets in our solar system, Jupiter has the strongest gravity, which is part of the reason Jupiter has almost 100 moons. If you weighed 100 pounds on Earth, you'd weigh 240 pounds on Jupiter because the force of gravity on Jupiter is 2.4 times stronger than on Earth.

The planet with the lowest gravity is Mercury. As the smallest planet in our solar system, it has a weak pull compared to gas giants like Jupiter. If you weighed 100 pounds on Earth, you'd only weigh 38 pounds on Mercury.

OLDEST AND YOUNGEST

Since the universe itself is billions of years old, the difference between the youngest and oldest objects is extremely big. Measuring the exact age of a celestial body isn't easy, so most ages you read about are just estimates and could change in the future as technology advances.

OLDEST AND YOUNGEST STARS

The oldest known star in the universe is called HD 140283, or "Methuselah." Scientists originally believed the star formed about 14.3 billion years ago. That confused many experts, since it would make Methuselah older than the universe itself! Over time, researchers reduced the age of Methuselah to around 12 million years old. However, its age still raises questions about the true beginning of the universe.

Though these old stars are fascinating, scientists are just as interested in learning about new ones. In 2020, astronomers discovered the youngest neutron star ever found. At the time, it was only 33 years old. Scientists knew the star's age because they'd been watching the supernova where it formed, SN 1987A, which is only 168,000 light-years away from Earth.

GALAXIES OLD AND NEW

In 2022, the James Webb Space Telescope discovered the GLASS-z13 galaxy, the oldest known galaxy in the universe. GLASS-z13 formed up to 13.5 billion years ago, and it's about 33.2 billion light-years from Earth.

The previous record holder for the oldest galaxy was GN-z11, which was discovered by the Hubble Space Telescope. As you can see, new technology helps astronomers make new discoveries by looking farther into the universe—that's why many of these records were set within the past decade.

The youngest known galaxy was found in 2023, but its age is a little confusing to understand. Because it takes so long for light to travel from galaxies that are far away, the way we see it from Earth isn't up to date. Think of it like taking a picture of yourself and sending to someone else; by the time they look at the picture, you've already aged a little bit in the time it took them to see the image. This effect is pretty extreme when it takes 13 billion years to send a message!

On Earth, the galaxy Abell2744_Y1 looks like it's only 650 million years younger than the Big Bang, which makes it the youngest known galaxy in the entire universe. In reality, it's 13 billion years older than that, but scientists on Earth aren't able to see far enough to determine its actual age.

ANCIENT METEORITES AND "BABY" ASTEROIDS

The Erg Chech 002 is the oldest meteorite ever found on Earth. It was discovered in 2020 in Algeria, and scientists believe it fell to Earth around 100 years ago. After studying the meteorite, experts realized that Erg Chech 2002 is unique compared to other meteorites — it may have been part of a developing planet that broke apart long ago.

The Imilac is another ancient meteorite that's estimated to be 4.5 billion years old. The meteor exploded over northern Chile and landed in the Atacama Desert, and scientists believe it was part of a larger meteor that originally weighed over 2,200 pounds!

In 2019, when 2019 PR2 and 2019 PR6 passed by Earth, astronomers were excited to realize that they were the youngest pair of asteroids ever discovered. Scientists believe they separated from a larger asteroid about 300 years ago. Before they were discovered, the youngest asteroid pair was 10 times older than 2019 PR2 and 2019 PR6.

One of these asteroids is about 3,280 feet across, while the other is half as wide, and they're separated by approximately 600,000 miles. Though that may seem like a lot, they're extremely close together for two objects in space. Their orbits around the sun are also similar.

CHAPTER SEVEN: SPACE EXPLORATION ACHIEVEMENTS

Space exploration is a team effort that involves astronauts, ground support, and all kinds of scientists. Many of these people are famous for their inventions and achievements. Certain missions and events have made it into popular culture, too, as everyday people learn more about the history of space exploration.

The internet has made it easier than ever to keep up with what's happening in space. Between April 2014 and July 2019, it was even possible to stream a live view of the Earth through a camera on the outside of the International Space Station! These programs truly show how far NASA has come since it was founded in 1958.

PIONEERS AND TRAILBLAZERS

We've already introduced many astronauts who became famous by setting records, surviving dangerous missions, or making new discoveries about space. However, it's also important to celebrate astronauts who did incredible things even when others doubted them because of things like their gender, race, or age. These amazing individuals didn't let anything hold them back as they followed their dreams to explore space.

THE FIRST WOMEN IN SPACE

The Russian astronaut Valentina Tereshkova was the first woman in space. She spent over 70 hours in space after launching on June 16, 1963, on the *Vostok 6*. Tereshkova worked in a textile factory and enjoyed skydiving in her free time. When she heard the Soviet Union was looking for astronauts, she applied and was chosen from a group of more than 400 candidates.

The first American woman to travel into space was Dr. Sally Ride. Unlike Tereshkova, Dr. Ride had a strong scientific background from studying physics at Stanford University. She joined NASA in 1978 as one of the first six women to become astronauts. On June 18, 1983, she flew on the seventh space shuttle mission, STS-7, and stayed in space for over six days. When Dr. Ride passed away in 2012, the world learned that she was also the first LGBTQIA+ astronaut.

Liu Yang was the first Chinese woman to fly in space. She started her career as a pilot in the People's Liberation Army. After flying cargo planes for over 20 years, she was selected to become an astronaut in 2010. Yang went into space on June 16, 2012, on the *Shenzhou 9*. She was in charge of carrying out medical experiments during the mission.

ASTRONAUTS OF COLOR

Arnaldo Tamayo Méndez joined the Cuban military as a pilot in March 1978. He went on to become the first Cuban and the first Latin American astronaut when he flew aboard *Soyuz 38* and the Soviet Union's *Salyut-6* space station in September 1980, spending eight days in space.

On June 17, 1985, Sultan ibn Salman Al Saud became the first Arab, Muslim, royal, and Saudi Arabian citizen to go into space. After being selected by NASA, he flew on the space shuttle *Discovery* for a week-long mission with six other astronauts. He also filmed the interior of the shuttle, narrating in Arabic so viewers in the Middle East could follow along with the mission.

Franklin R. Chang-Díaz was the first Hispanic American in space. He was assigned to the STS-61C mission on the space shuttle *Columbia*, which launched in January 1986. The crew spent six days in space, launching a communications satellite and studying Halley's comet. Chang-Díaz flew an additional six times and spent over 1,600 hours total in space. He shares the record for the most missions ever flown with Jerry Ross.

Dr. Mae Jemison, a doctor who spent time in the Peace Corps, was the first Black woman in space, launching onboard the space shuttle *Endeavour* on September 12, 1992. She spent eight days in space and orbited the Earth 127 times. During the mission, she conducted experiments on bone loss and motion sickness to learn more about how spaceflight affects the human body.

John Herrington, a member of the Chickasaw Nation, became the first Indigenous astronaut to go into space on November 23, 2002. He launched on the space shuttle *Endeavour* as part of the STS-113 mission and traveled to the International Space Station, spending a total of 13 days in space.

OLDEST AND YOUNGEST

John Glenn, the first astronaut to orbit the Earth, also holds the record for the oldest astronaut in space. On October 29, 1998, he completed a mission onboard the space shuttle *Discovery* at the age of 77. Over the course of nine days, he helped scientists at NASA study how an older person's body behaves in space.

However, John Glenn's record as the oldest astronaut in space only applies to professionals. On October 13, 2021, the Canadian actor William Shatner became the oldest person to travel into space when he boarded a tourist flight at the age of 90 years old. Shatner, of course, is famous for playing Captain Kirk in the Star Trek series. Before going on the flight, he practiced in simulations and training exercises to make sure he was healthy enough for the trip.

The record for the youngest person in space is also divided between professionals and tourists. Gherman Titov holds the record for the youngest professional astronaut. He orbited the Earth on August 6, 1961, aboard the Soviet Union's *Vostok 2* a month before turning 26. He was the fourth person in space after Yuri Gagarin, Alan Shepard, and Gus Grissom.

On August 10, 2023, 18-year-old space tourist Anastatia Mayers set a record as the youngest person to ever go into space. Since she was accompanied by her mother, they also share the record for being the first Caribbean women and the first mother–daughter duo aboard any spacecraft in history.

FUNNY FIRSTS

Learning about space takes a lot of creativity, so some records and achievements are a little strange. Setting unusual goals and attempting new things gives space agencies the chance to discover more about what it's like to live in orbit. Think about how many different tasks and actions you do every day—for people in space, they might be setting a record just by eating a new food or putting on their favorite song!

MOVING AN ASTEROID

Crashing on purpose sounds like a strange thing to do, but that's exactly what happened in 2022, when NASA decided to test whether it would be possible to redirect an asteroid by crashing into it. Asteroids don't get to choose where they go, and several have ended up hitting Earth in the past.

For example, an asteroid struck the planet around two billion years ago and left behind the Vredefort Crater in South Africa. Researchers believe the crater was up to 186 miles wide when it was first formed. An asteroid of that size would cause a major disaster in today's world. Instead of waiting until an asteroid looks like it might hit the planet again, NASA has started thinking of ways to protect the Earth before that happens.

The Double Asteroid Redirection Test, or DART, took place on September 26, 2022. DART launched from a base in California to hit Dimorphos, an asteroid that was about 6.8 million miles from Earth at that time. Crashing DART into Dimorphos changed the asteroid's shape and orbit. Instead of being round, it now has a more oval shape and completes an orbit 33 minutes faster than it did before.

FISH IN SPACE

Medaka, also known as "Japanese rice fish," were sent into space as part of an experiment to learn more about bone loss. Medaka have transparent skin, so it's easier for astronauts to see how they grow and develop. Four fish were sent for the first mission in 1994.

These fish became so important that the International Space Station installed an aquarium in 2012. The aquarium is maintained by the Japan Aerospace Exploration Agency on the Kibo module. With the right support, Medaka can live for up to 90 days and have even reproduced in space!

THE FIRST PIZZA DELIVERY IN SPACE

Believe it or not, there's already been a pizza delivery to outer space. In March 2001, Pizza Hut loaded a six-inch pizza onto a resupply rocket for the International Space Station. Instead of pepperoni, Pizza Hut used salami as a topping since it worked the best in testing, and the astronauts heated the pizza up using the oven on the ISS.

SNOOPY THE ASTRONAUT

In 1968, Snoopy the cartoon dog became a mascot for NASA's Manned Flight Awareness program. Before long, posters with Snoopy could be found throughout NASA facilities. The goal of the program was to remind NASA employees to do everything they could to keep astronauts safe.

Later that year, the crew of *Apollo 8* took Snoopy pins on their mission to the moon, creating a tradition that NASA personnel would follow for decades to come. Other astronauts took Snoopy items on the space shuttle *Columbia* STS-32, and Snoopy went to the International Space Station in 2019.

When *Artemis I* went to the moon in late 2022, Snoopy was an important part of the mission. A stuffed Snoopy plushie served as the zero-gravity indicator, small items that float to show when a spacecraft has entered microgravity. NASA even created a suit for Snoopy out of same material worn by real astronauts!

UNUSUAL FINDS

Scientists have only studied a small portion of our universe, so astronomers are always making new discoveries in space exploration, and not all of them are made on purpose. Sometimes, researchers find a new place or an unexpected object completely by accident!

These surprises can become the target of new missions or research projects in the future. Even if the group that made a discovery can't focus on it at the time, other scientists might be interested in learning more—that's why it's important for space agencies, universities, and private companies to work together instead of competing over a place as vast as outer space.

A ROGUE PLANET IN LIGHTS

In 2016, astronomers found a rogue planet about 20 light-years away from the sun and named it SIMP J01365663+0933473. A rogue planet isn't caught up in an orbit, so it floats from place to place. SIMP J01365663+0933473 is unique because it has a magnetic field that's four million times stronger than the one on Earth.

This rogue planet is also interesting because it produces bright auroras, similar to the northern lights on Earth and the auroras on Jupiter. However, scientists don't know what causes the lights on SIMP J01365663+0933473. Earth's auroras come from the sun, while Jupiter's are caused by its moon Io, so it's possible that SIMP J01365663+0933473 has a moon that researchers have yet to find.

COSMIC EXPLOSIONS

Astronomers accidentally discovered the largest cosmic explosion ever observed while conducting research in 2023. Named AT2021lwx, the explosion created a ball of fire 100 times bigger than our solar system! Scientists estimate that the fireball started burning around three years before it was spotted by the Zwicky Transient Facility in California. AT2021lwx is about eight billion light-years away from Earth.

Astronomers are still trying to understand what caused this explosion. Even though it's up to two trillion times brighter than the sun, it isn't the brightest flash in the universe—that award belongs to a gamma-ray burst that's been nicknamed the BOAT—the Brightest of All Time.

EUROPA'S ICY OCEAN

When *Voyager 1* and *Voyager 2* took images of Jupiter's moon Europa in 1979, experts were surprised to see potential signs of water. They even changed the *Galileo* mission that launched in 1989 so it could get more information about Europa. *Galileo* flew by Europa 12 times and took measurements that indicated that saltwater could exist. This matched up with what scientists thought after seeing the pictures from *Voyager 1* and *Voyager 2*.

Eventually, *Galileo* ran out of fuel, so NASA decided to crash the probe into Jupiter on September 21, 2003, to make sure it couldn't cause any damage to Europa. However, the agency started planning future missions to the area.

One of these, the *Europa Clipper*, is due to reach Jupiter by 2030. Its plan is to fly over Europa close to 50 times and scan different parts of the moon each time. The European Space Agency's *Jupiter Icy Moons Explorer* (Juice) will arrive in 2031 to study Ganymede, Callisto, and Europa.

COSMIC ACCIDENTS

Despite the many achievements made by space organizations around the world, there have been plenty of mistakes. Instead of thinking of these mistakes as failures, scientists learn from them and keep improving to make sure they don't happen again.

DESTROYING A MARS ORBITER

During the 1990s, NASA changed how it built space probes. Before this, probes were built with all types of specialized gadgets to take measurements in space. In 1994, the administrator of NASA wanted to create probes that were smaller and cheaper, which would allow NASA to build more probes and use them for specific reasons. It's a little like having a smartphone with a calculator app or just having a calculator by itself—if all you want to do is add some numbers, do you really need the whole smartphone?

Years later, the Jet Propulsion Laboratory partnered with a company called Lockheed Martin Astronautics to design the *Mars Climate Orbiter*. The project cost $125 million to complete. Unfortunately, NASA used metric units like millimeters, while Lockheed Martin Astronautics used English measurements like inches. This mistake meant that none of their math added up.

No one knew about the problem when they launched the *Mars Climate Orbiter* on December 11, 1998. Everything seemed to be working fine until September 23, 1999, when the orbiter reached Mars and NASA realized something was wrong. The probe ended up traveling too close to the planet, and NASA declared the mission a failure two days later.

FIXING THE HUBBLE SPACE TELESCOPE

Shortly after the Hubble Space Telescope launched in 1990, NASA realized there was something wrong with one of its mirrors. The images taken by the Hubble's camera were blurry. NASA investigated the problem and learned that one of the mirrors had the wrong shape — it was too flat on one part of the curve.

Humans can have a similar problem with their eyes, which is why some people wear glasses to help them see. NASA built the Corrective Optics Space Telescope Axial Replacement to fix Hubble's "vision." This tool was installed in December 1993, when the first mission arrived to check on the telescope.

LOSING A TOOL BAG

On November 2, 2023, two astronauts were on a spacewalk outside the International Space Station when they lost control of a tool bag. The bag was drawn into orbit around the Earth, just a short distance in front of the ISS.

As it gets closer to Earth, the bag will eventually be destroyed as. Astronomers believe it will disintegrate once it's within 70 miles of the planet. Until that point, stargazers will be able to see the bag from Earth's surface using a telescope.

A similar issue arose in 2008, when astronaut Heidemarie Stefanyshyn-Piper was trying to clean grease from inside her tool bag. The bag slipped out of her grasp and floated away. She thought about trying to jump and grab it, but decided it was too dangerous. Even though the bag was worth $100,000, trying to retrieve it wasn't worth the risk.

CHAPTER EIGHT: SPACE FUN AND ACTIVITIES

Learning about space can mesh with other activities and hobbies such as hiking, art, and movies. Even something as simple as adding space-themed stickers to your school folders can remind you of your favorite subject throughout the day!

If you have friends who enjoy hearing about astronauts and outer space, there are plenty of group activities you can try together. Most people have at least some interest in learning about the universe, so it shouldn't be hard to get others involved. Whether you host a movie night or bring a board game to a sleepover, you can always find a way to share your love of space exploration.

In addition, your school might have activities to help you learn more about space. If not, ask if other students want to make a new after-school club. Many schools will let you start a club if you have a teacher to help, and virtual options can allow you to join kids from all over the country.

As you get older, you'll have more control over the classes you take, and some schools offer robotics classes and other electives that have ties with space exploration. Even if you just study biology or chemistry, learning more about the world around you will make it easier to learn about missions and atmospheric tests.

STARGAZING TIPS

It's easy to start stargazing—all you need to do is go outside! While it helps to have equipment, you don't need it to see the brightest constellations and planets. There may even be times that you can see special events like meteor showers.

Which stars you'll be able to see depends on where you're located, as some stars are only visible in certain parts of the world. If you aren't sure what to look for, do some research ahead of time. In the northern hemisphere, for example, it's usually easy to spot the Big Dipper and the North Star.

EQUIPMENT TO GET STARTED

Though you've read a lot about advanced equipment, such as the James Webb Space Telescope, you don't need fancy equipment to stargaze from home. In fact, you can see plenty of constellations with just your eyes—after all, that's how early astronomers studied the stars before telescopes were even invented!

If you do decide to get a telescope, it's okay to start with a simple model. That will help you learn what you like before you buy a more advanced one. Many basic telescopes come with upgrades and accessories. For example, the Celestron AstroMaster LT 60AZ Refractor is sold with multiple eyepieces and a tripod. It even has an attachment to hold a smartphone and take pictures.

Besides a telescope, it's also a good idea to buy a notebook to write down what you've seen. You can even draw the constellations you've already found or make a list of what you want to search for next. After you've gained more experience with stargazing, you can look back at your journal to see how much you've accomplished.

Lastly, you may want to get a waterproof tarp or a beach towel to add to your stargazing kit. It gets cold at night, and it's nice to have a dry place to put your equipment or sit down while you're watching the stars.

STARGAZING APPS

Apps like *Stellarium Mobile* and *Star Walk 2* can help you identify constellations when you point your phone's camera at the sky. They even draw the shape of the constellation on top—for instance, Ursa Major will look like a bear.

Some apps also mark satellites and other human-made objects in space. NASA has its own tool, *Spot the Station*, for following the International Space Station. *Spot the Station*'s map allows you to look up sighting opportunities for your area. It also shows how fast the ISS is moving and its altitude.

THE BEST LOCATIONS FOR STARGAZING

The best places to stargaze are dark areas, away from cities and highways. Locations with a higher elevation are even better, since you won't have to worry about fog and mist interfering with your view. Not everyone lives close to a place that matches this description, so don't be too upset if you don't have the perfect spot.

Even if you live in a city, you can search for open areas without a lot of trees or buildings nearby. A park or an open field could both work. One direction might be better than another, especially if there are lights around you. The weather also makes a huge difference in how much you'll be able to see, so try to choose a night that isn't cloudy or rainy.

If you can travel, you may be able to find an International Dark Sky Place (IDSP). These areas are famous for their stargazing, due to the lack of light from cities and roads, and there are 138 IDSPs in the United States. Many of them are in state or national parks, where there's open land without many buildings. For example, Arches National Park in Utah and Big Bend National Park in Texas both make the list.

Even if you can't head out to an IDSP, moving away from the city will make it easier to see the stars. Going camping for a weekend or taking a late drive with your loved ones can give you the chance to spot different constellations or objects that might not be visible from where you live.

SPACE CRAFTS

Hands-on activities allow you to combine your love of space with arts and crafts. The projects in this book aren't too complicated, without any special rules—the important part is to have fun and use your creativity! Your friends or family members may even want to join in and share what they know about outer space.

BUILDING MODELS

Building your own model of the solar system is a fun way to see all the planets together. Most craft stores sell foam balls that you can paint to look like each planet. When you're finished, put the planets on a mat and label their orbits to create a map of the solar system. You can also use wooden sticks to hold up your planets if you want to make a model with more of a 3D feel.

If you're more interested in things that humans have sent to space, it's easy to build simple models using tinfoil, popsicle sticks, glue, and toilet paper rolls. Just look up a picture of your favorite rover or other piece of equipment to get some ideas about what to build. For example, you can use popsicle sticks for solar panels on the International Space Station.

Putting together LEGO kits is another fun activity for space enthusiasts. LEGO has an entire series of models involving space exploration. From rovers to space shuttles, building LEGO kits let you indulge your love of space in a hands-on way without requiring as many additional supplies as other arts and crafts.

DRAWING THE SOLAR SYSTEM

You don't need special lessons to draw pictures of space. You can draw different parts of the universe from your own imagination or by looking up real pictures from space telescopes. Drawing is also a great way to study constellations and see how the stars fit together to form different shapes.

However, if you feel more comfortable having a guide, the "Art for Kids Hub" on *YouTube* offers a series called *How to Draw Space: The Art for Kids Hub Guide to the Galaxy*. These videos will show you how to draw everything from a telescope to a solar eclipse. For less scientific drawings, there are even tutorials on how to draw silly space aliens and cartoon versions of the sun.

COLORING PAGES

If you prefer coloring, *NASA Space Place* has free coloring sheets online that you can download and print at home. Each page includes fun facts about planets, moons, and NASA missions. Coloring pictures of Mars rovers like *Curiosity* can also help you understand what each rover looked like in real life.

NASA Space Place also has other scientific coloring pages, if you want to learn more about the water cycle or carbon dioxide. While these topics aren't directly space related, astronomers still need to understand other subjects like biology in order to study other planets.

STICKER AND ART BOOKS

Sticker books aren't just for young kids! *Discovery*, *Paint by Sticker*, and *Brain Games* all make space-themed sticker books for older kids. Many sticker books are designed like color-by-number projects, but you don't have to worry about getting other art supplies — they use stickers instead of paint or markers.

LUNAR DESSERTS

Another fun activity is to draw the phases of the moon on chocolate cookies or cupcakes, using white frosting to outline the different shapes. If that's too difficult, you can also buy chocolate cookie sandwiches and separate them, so you only have the side with the cream frosting on top. Then, use a spoon to scrape away some of the cream filling until you have the right shape for each phase of the moon.

SPACE GAMES AND PUZZLES

Games and puzzles about space can challenge you to apply what you know about space exploration. Many activities are designed for more than one person, in case you want to play along with siblings, friends, or classmates. In addition, even more options for games are available online and on gaming consoles.

CARD AND BOARD GAMES

For groups, card games, such as *Guess in 10* by Skillmatics, give you the chance to show off your knowledge of space. The rules for *Guess in 10* are easy to follow: One person draws a card without showing it to anyone else. Then, another player can ask up to 10 questions to figure out which planet, piece of equipment, or other space-related object is on their card. The deck includes pictures from NASA and can be played with up to six people.

You may also be able to find your favorite board games in a space theme. *Risk: Deep Space*, *Monopoly: Night Sky*, and space-themed bingo cards are just a few options. While these don't teach you anything new about space, they can still remind you of your favorite subjects while you play with friends and loved ones.

PUZZLES

Jigsaw puzzles are a simple way to enjoy art and work your brain at the same time. It should be easy to find puzzles with generic space themes such as aliens, rockets, or astronauts—some puzzle companies even have permission from NASA to use their logo and designs. These puzzles feature images of real NASA spacecraft and pictures taken by space telescopes or probes. NASA headquarters and the NASA Johnson Space Center both sell puzzles through their official stores.

If you're looking for a more challenging activity, three-dimensional puzzles come in all shapes and sizes. They're usually made of foam, plastic, or another sturdy material to help them stick together. It's even possible to build round puzzles in the shape of different planets! Once you're finished, you can keep the completed puzzle to display it.

VIDEO GAMES AND VIRTUAL REALITY

If you'd rather play video games, all you need is a computer. *NASA Space Place* offers a few basic online games. In *CubeSat Builder*, you get to help build spacecraft at NASA. Meanwhile, *Explore Mars* gives you the chance to drive a Mars rover and collect samples from the surface. Charlene Pfeifer, the narrator of *Explore Mars*, is a real NASA systems engineer who's worked on missions to Mars.

For something a bit more advanced, the Meta Quest VR headset supports several space-related games and virtual experiences.

Mission: ISS is a free virtual experience that lets you explore the International Space Station in a more detailed way. You can even go on a spacewalk or dock a space capsule! *Apollo 11* is a paid experience that walks you through the mission, including video and audio footage from the real spacecraft.

SPACE QUIZZES

Taking quizzes about space is another way to discover what you might want to learn about next. If you don't know the answer to a question, it gives you something new to investigate. Kidzworld, National Geographic Kids, and Guinness World Record Kids all have astronomy and space-related quizzes on their websites.

SPACE BOOKS AND MOVIES

Reading other books about space and watching movies gives you the chance to learn even more about the universe. Some focus on specific topics like a particular mission, while others contain more general information about space. Choosing a variety of different books and movies will expose you to new areas of space exploration.

You may eventually discover that you love one part of space more than others. If you want to find more books and movies on that subject, ask an adult for help. Your parents, guardians, or teachers may know where to find more materials about your favorite topic.

Your local library also likely has a section of books and movies dedicated to space exploration.

SPACE BOOKS

The Smithsonian Institute publishes a visual encyclopedia that includes images from NASA and the European Space Agency. Diagrams, panels, and timelines provide you with a new way to think of different topics, even if you know a little about them already. This encyclopedia also includes interviews and suggested activities.

If you'd rather learn from people, several former astronauts have written books about their experiences. Terry Virts, NASA astronaut and a former commander of the International Space Station, wrote a book called *The Astronaut's Guide to Leaving the Planet*. For questions about spaceflight, there's also *Ask the Astronaut* by Tom Jones, who spent over 53 days in space over four space shuttle missions.

Your local librarian may also be able to help you find books about space. Most libraries have entire sections with books about science, but it might be tricky to figure out which ones are about space exploration if they're mixed in with other subjects. If there's a book you really want to read that isn't on the shelves, ask your librarian if they can order it or request it from another library in your area.

MOVIES AND SHOWS

There are dozens of movies and shows about different aspects of space. You might be able to view some of these online, while others will only be available on certain streaming services. For example, the show *Space Kids* on Kidstream explains important topics, such as light-years and mission control. You'll see real pictures of the planets and helpful drawings that make it easier to understand ideas like microgravity.

For movies, *Journey to Space* was released in 2005 and contains real footage from missions. This documentary is a great way to learn about the history of space exploration and major missions that took place before 2005. Meanwhile, *Zero Gravity* follows a group of middle-schoolers from California as they enter a NASA competition to code satellites on the International Space Station.

Besides documentaries, you can also find plenty of fictional stories and movies based on real missions. For example, the story of the *Apollo 13* crisis was made into an award-winning movie in 1995, starring some of the biggest actors of the time. If you think back to the section on *Apollo 13*, you'll remember that this mission to the moon experienced an emergency when an oxygen tank exploded. Astronauts James Lovell, Fred Haise, and John "Jack" Swigert worked with NASA experts on the ground to make it home safely.

VIDEOS AND SHORTS

YouTube is a great place to find space-themed videos that aren't as long as regular shows or movies. NASA's official channel features live video of the International Space Station and a live stream of NASA TV. It also has videos about lunar terrain vehicles, life as an astronaut, and dozens of other topics.

Similarly, the European Space Agency has its own channel with videos about different missions and events. You can watch recordings of launch tests, watch astronauts graduate from training, and see footage from the ESA's Euclid space telescope.

SPACE PARTIES AND EVENTS

Many people throw parties to celebrate their personal hobbies — for example, it's common to invite friends and family over for sporting events like the Super Bowl. You can do the same thing to watch spacecraft launch or witness a natural phenomenon. During the 2024 solar eclipse, the entire town of St. Johnsbury, Vermont, threw a party to watch and celebrate.

DECORATIONS

One of the best parts of having a party at home is being able to choose the decorations. From aliens to rockets, you don't have to hold back when it's time for a party! Here are some ideas to get you started:

- Tablecloths, plates, and napkins with stars or planets

- Cupcakes or cookies with space-themed frosting

- Black balloons painted with specks to look like stars

- Astronaut or robot figurines

- Banners with the NASA logo

- Freeze-dried ice cream

Not all decorations from the store will be the most accurate, so if you want your decorations to match actual NASA equipment, you'll have to get creative. Printing real pictures of equipment or the planets can help your party look more official. If you've made any art projects about outer space, you can add them to the rest of your decorations to show off your work.

COSTUMES FROM SPACE

There are more opportunities to wear space costumes than you might think. You can dress up for occasions like Halloween or have a costume party for your birthday. Your school might also have a career day where you're allowed to dress up. If you don't want to be an astronaut, but you're still interested in space exploration, try dressing up as a member of mission control or an astronomer.

Some school projects also give you the chance to pick your own topics or research any historical figure. If you choose a famous astronomer like Galileo or an astronaut like Dr. Mae Jemison, your teacher might let you dress up to present your project to the class.

SPACE MUSIC

Did you know there's even music dedicated to space? Between 1914 and 1917, the English composer Gustav Holst wrote an orchestral suite called *The Planets* that has seven different movements. Each part is dedicated to a different planet. For example, since Mars is named after Roman god of war, the section about Mars is faster and louder than other movements.

You can also search online for *Space Sessions: Songs from a Tin Can*, the first album recorded in space. Astronaut Chris Hadfield recorded it while serving as the commander of the International Space Station in 2013. He had to play his guitar inside his sleep pod to keep the noise from interfering. Adding this music to your party or event can make your theme stand out even more.

CONCLUSION

Congratulations on reaching the end of this book! We've covered so many amazing facts about space exploration and what the future might hold as we journey farther into the universe. Hopefully, you've read about a few missions or scientific ideas to research in greater detail on your own.

There will always be new things to learn as NASA and other space agencies explore different parts of the universe, and you'll have opportunities to see natural phenomena like eclipses from time to time. Whether you end up becoming a professional astronaut or you just want to study the stars for fun, your interest in space can follow you for the rest of your life.

The important thing is to stay curious and always be open to new theories. As technology gets more advanced, researchers are making new discoveries faster than ever before. Of course, sometimes it's hard to let go of things we used to believe as things change. For example, many people are still upset that Pluto was demoted as a planet.

However, keeping an open mind is a huge part of being a scientist. You never know when we'll discover another planet like Earth or figure out a new law about the universe. We might even see astronauts going to Mars for the first time during this next age of space exploration! No matter what the future holds for NASA and other space agencies around the world, you now have the knowledge you'll need to track missions, study distant planets, and follow along with the latest discoveries in space. Good luck!

Made in United States
Cleveland, OH
03 December 2024

10997276R00079